JAWS!

Tracy's hair was a mess, and there was a smudge of dirt on her nose. She was shaken up, but seemed to be unharmed.

"Really, Tracy, there's plenty of room for you up front," James said, helping her out of the car trunk where she'd been locked for hours. "Are you okay?"

"No!" All the blood rushed from Tracy's face as she pointed over James's shoulder. "There he is! The man who kidnapped me!"

James spun around. "Jaws," he whispered.

In the doorway stood the hulking, shadowy figure of the S.C.U.M. agent. The huge man smiled, his metal teeth sparkling.

"It's dinner time," he said, stepping into the van. "And *you're* dinner!"

This is for John Peel, who helped fill in all the blanks.

A View to a Thrill

John Vincent

PUFFIN BOOKS

PUFFIN BOOKS
Published by the Penguin Group
Viking Penguin, a division of Penguin Books USA Inc.,
375 Hudson Street, New York, New York 10014, U.S.A.
Penguin Books Ltd, 27 Wrights Lane, London W8 5TZ, England
Penguin Books Australia Ltd, Ringwood, Victoria, Australia
Penguin Books Canada Ltd, 10 Alcorn Avenue, Toronto, Ontario, Canada M4V 3B2
Penguin Books (N.Z.) Ltd, 182–190 Wairau Road, Auckland 10, New Zealand

Penguin Books Ltd, Registered Offices: Harmondsworth, Middlesex, England

First published in the United States of America by Puffin Books,
a division of Penguin Books USA Inc., 1992

1 3 5 7 9 10 8 6 4 2

Library of Congress Catalog Card Number: 91-66672
ISBN: 0-14-036011-5

Printed in the United States of America
Set in Cheltenham Book

A View to a Thrill

Chapter One
Car Trouble

TOP SECRET MESSAGE FROM M TO 007: E.M.P. DEVICE HAS BEEN INSTALLED IN YOUR CAR. IT IS READY FOR YOU TO DELIVER AS INSTRUCTED.

TOP SECRET MESSAGE FROM 007 TO M: WILL DELIVER AS SOON AS POSSIBLE. TRUST THERE IS NO CONFUSION AS NEPHEW HAS BORROWED MY ASTON MARTIN TO GO TO HIS NEW SCHOOL.

It wouldn't be long now! James Bond Jr. checked the electronic map set in the car's dashboard. Outside, the English countryside flashed by as he sped along. Blip! Blip! The map automatically kept up. As the blinking light tracked his progress, Bond could easily see his route and where he was in relation to it.

His turnoff was coming up soon. *I'm late enough*

as it is, he thought. *I better not miss it.* He shifted gears, feeling the powerful engine surge inside the Aston Martin sports car. James knew the car was old, but it was still the best as far as he was concerned. Behind the wheel of the sleek, low-slung silver car, he knew he could beat just about anything.

There it was! With a screech of burning rubber, James swung the wheel hard. The car shot into the narrow road. A low stone wall ran on either side, and there were only inches to spare.

The dust kicked up by the silver Aston Martin had barely settled when a jet-black Rolls-Royce flew into the turn. Its tires screamed and the left fender scraped loudly against the stone wall, ripping a deep scratch in the midnight-black finish of the Rolls. Then the tires gripped the road, and the car swung away from the wall.

The Rolls's driver swore under his breath, shaking his dented head, which looked as though it had been smashed with a hammer. He had a bumpy face, and his nose was crooked and red. His body was shaped like a gorilla's, wide and squat. Muscles bulged everywhere as he grabbed the gear stick with his left hand and flicked open the top, exposing a red button. He pressed the button once and a small target appeared on the windshield. As he moved the stick, the target followed it. Squinting his beady eyes, he centered the target on the Aston Martin and pressed the button again.

With a faint hum, a thin barrel emerged from the front grille of the Rolls-Royce. Using the gear lever, the driver lined up the barrel on the fleeing Aston Martin. An evil smile spread across his ugly face as he pressed the firing button.

As the Rolls swerved around a bend in the road a laser beam shot from it. Instead of slicing the silver car to pieces, the beam slammed into the roadside wall. In a blast of sparks several of the rocks shattered, raining dust and chips all over the road. Fragments of the wall bounced off the hood of the Rolls, speckling the paint with dents and scratches.

The driver groaned. Not only had he missed the target, but his boss would kill him for ruining the beautiful car. In the back seat, the mastermind hissed to himself and petted his pit bull's head. But he said nothing.

Pulling hard on the steering wheel, the driver followed the Aston Martin around the bend, teetering on two wheels.

"Careful, you clod!" the man in the back seat snapped.

Swallowing nervously, the driver nodded. "Sure thing, boss," he promised. Then he lined up the laser cannon again.

This time he wouldn't miss!

Inside the Aston Martin, the driver had a faint smile on his lips. The Rolls could never catch him. These roads were too narrow; sooner or later he'd get away.

Suddenly an alarm started to beep. Glancing down at the panel set in between the two front seats, he saw a number of lights and switches. One red light was flashing on and off.

"Laser beam!" He laughed. "So they want to play games?"

He flicked one of the switches on the panel, then reached down to change the cassette in the tape player. He didn't care for the classical music it had been playing. A rock-and-roll guitar riff burst from the speakers, and he nodded in satisfaction. Much better!

As the Rolls bounced along the rough road, the driver snarled and aimed the laser beam for a second shot. As soon as the Aston Martin was in line, he pressed the firing button. A fiery beam shot out, heading straight for the rear window of the silver car. Automatically, a long panel just behind the rear window opened in the Aston Martin, and a shield of solid metal whined upward to protect the glass. The laser beam hit the shield in a sparkle of color. Like a mirror, the highly polished metal sent the beam back at the Rolls.

The beam sliced through the grille and fender of the Rolls like a knife through butter. Spraying sparks and smoke, the laser cannon exploded. Blinded by the blast, the driver couldn't keep the car on the road. It swerved, skidded, and slammed into the stone barricade. The Rolls broke through the wall and bounced into the field beyond. The driver hit the brakes, slowing the car down until he could get it under control again.

The once-beautiful car was covered with holes and dents. Parts of the trim were missing, and a lot of the paint. There was a large crack in the windshield, and the laser cannon swung crazily inside the shattered grille. Far ahead of them, the Aston Martin followed the road curving back toward the field in which the Rolls had landed.

The back-seat passenger hissed angrily, then pointed. "Cut across the field, you idiot, and get ahead of him!" The animal on his lap growled, and snapped his jaws open and shut several times.

The driver sent the Rolls roaring across the muddy field, spraying dirty water in its wake, and scaring the small herd of cows trying to eat their lunch. Directly in front of the Rolls, a barbed-wire fence blocked the entrance to the road. The driver crouched low in his seat and pushed down hard on the gas pedal.

Smashing into the gate, the Rolls shattered it and sent bits of wood and wire flying all around them. One post banged noisily off the roof, scraping off even more of the car's paint. Fighting the steering wheel, the driver managed to get the car back on the road. The Aston Martin was still ahead of them, but they were right on its tail now.

Both cars flashed around the next bend in the road.

Directly ahead of them, the road was completely blocked by a huge eighteen-wheel truck and a farmer on his tractor. James Bond Jr. glanced in the rearview mirror of his uncle's Aston Martin. The Rolls was still close behind him. James caught sight of his own reflection, too: not at all a bad face for a seventeen-year-old student. But a bit on the young side for a secret agent.

Not that he really was a secret agent, but it sure seemed like these guys tailing him thought he was. He knew that his uncle, the James Bond he was named after—Double-O-Seven—was a famous agent of the British Secret Service. People often told James how much he looked like his uncle, and James secretly hoped the resemblance went deeper than just good looks. But he hadn't expected that driving the car Double-O-Seven had loaned him to get to his new school would get *this* dangerous!

"I've either got some serious trouble on my tail," he said to himself, "or my new headmaster *really* doesn't like people who are tardy." He hadn't meant to be late to his first day of school, but there had been a pretty French girl hitchhiking to Dover, and it really hadn't been that far out of his way. And she'd looked so lonely standing out on the road. . . . He wondered how long the Rolls had been following him before it had made its move.

It was bad enough being shot at with a laser beam and chased all over the English countryside. Now he was speeding straight toward a roadblock made from a tractor and a car transporter, with no room to stop and no way off the road except into a solid stone wall.

Well, as his uncle always said, what you can't go around, go over. . . .

He shifted into high gear and slammed his foot down to the floor. The Aston Martin sprang forward, the speedometer reading almost ninety miles an hour. At the last second, just when it looked as if he'd hit the tractor, he gave the steering wheel a quick turn and prayed he'd worked this one out right. . . .

The car shot up the ramp of the transporter. Instead of it simply rolling onto the flat back of the truck, the Aston Martin took off, sailing over the roof of the truck. Then it fell back to the road with a loud thud and shook so violently that James was almost thrown out of his seat. Luckily his safety belt held firm. He downshifted and sped away, spraying gravel behind him.

James looked in the rearview mirror again. The driver of the Rolls was trying to copy his escape. James shook his head. Didn't they realize that the Rolls was much heavier than the Aston Martin? They'd never be able to. . . .

The Rolls shot up the ramp. But instead of launching into the air, it fell forward, shooting down the flat back of the truck right into the cab of the transporter. In a scream of grinding metal, the cab was crushed, and the front end of the Rolls flattened. Steam, smoke, and bits of flying metal filled the air.

James laughed at the sight in his rearview mirror. "I think they missed their flight," he joked.

He wondered who had been chasing him and why. Had someone mistaken him for his uncle? Were they after him, or possibly the car? He honestly had no idea, but at least for now he was out of trouble.

As he sped past a side road, two motorcycles roared out and onto his tail. Both bikes were black, and their riders wore leather outfits and helmets with dark tinted glass. The riders were bent low over their handlebars, pushing their bikes to go faster.

"Sunday drivers," James muttered to himself. Would there ever be an end to this?

The first biker twisted his throttle, and a sudden jet of flame shot out from the black piping that ran down the side of the bike. James realized it had fired a small missile at him. What on earth was going on?

With a sharp pull on the wheel, he sent the car spinning off the road, through a fence. As the wood shattered around him, he had a quick glimpse of a startled cow, and then an open field. From the road behind him came the sound of an explosion, and a blast of fiery smoke. The missile hadn't missed by much. The two bikes had followed him through the fence into the field. In a few seconds, they would have the car in their sights again!

His uncle had told him that the car was bulletproof. In the spy game, it had to be. But James didn't think it was missile-proof. . . . One good hit from those bikes, and he'd be history.

The Aston Martin flashed past a sign that said: CLIFF AHEAD—DANGER!!! James had just enough time to read it before the car sailed off the edge of the cliff.

The two bikers saw the sign and pulled over hard on their machines, skidding to a halt in a shower of pebbles and clods of grass. They looked at each other, and then at the drop-off, just inches in front of them. They saw the churning waves and sharp rocks below. Bond couldn't possibly escape. He was doomed, and they had very nearly followed him.

Back in the road, the driver and passenger had clambered out of the shattered Rolls-Royce. While the driver stared at the mess, the other man put a pair of binoculars to his eyes. His face was hidden under the shadow of a large hat, but his lips could be seen curling into an evil sneer as he followed the fleeing Aston Martin's path as it fell off the cliff.

"Good-bye, Bond . . ." he whispered.

The man was dressed in a heavy coat and hat, even though it was a warm day. He was also wearing white gloves and dark glasses. Only his mouth could be seen, and it looked very cruel. He didn't seem to be aware of the farmer who was approaching to complain about the mess in his field. A warning growl made the farmer stop. He looked down. At the man's feet, hidden in the shadows of his long coat, was a stocky dog. It had a thick, squat head, swept-back ears, and a stub for a tail. The farmer knew it was one of those nasty-tempered American pit bulls the papers had been so filled with horror stories about. Didn't they eat people?

He took a step back. "Nice doggy," he said in a tiny voice.

The dog looked at him and growled, low and deep. It didn't like being called *nice*. . . .

James fought back his panic as the Aston Martin dove in a free-fall. He hit another of the control switches on the car's panels. This one was labeled FLIGHT CONVERSION. Then he closed his eyes after seeing the waves and rocks right below him.

Instantly, the car lurched. From beneath the doors, two wings folded out and snapped into place. A small tail fin rose from the trunk. The grille opened up and a small propeller emerged, coughed, and started to turn.

The steering wheel seemed looser in James's hands, and he pulled it hard toward his chest.

The nose of the Aston Martin rose, and the car-turned-airplane straightened out, skimming the waves as it came out of the dive.

James couldn't believe he was actually flying. In a car! Now he knew why his uncle loved his job so much. He could see the school on the cliffs in the

distance. If he was going to be late, he might as well give them an entrance they'd never forget.

The man in the hat threw down the binoculars, shattering them on the ground. "Blast it!" he yelled. Then he tore off his hat and threw it to the ground. "This isn't the end yet, Bond," he promised.

The pit bull eyed the hat and growled. Then it pounced, grabbed the hat in its sharp fangs, and tore it into tiny pieces. It was still growling and ripping when the ape-like driver came nervously over to join his passenger.

"The car's a total wreck, boss," he said.

"I can see that, you idiot!" the chief screamed. "I ought to rip you into as many pieces as that car is in!" For one second, it looked as if he just might try it. The driver, huge gorilla that he was, was actually shaking at the threat. Then the boss managed to get a hold on his temper. "But then I'd have to drive myself. You're lucky this time."

The driver nodded, knowing how true this was. "But—how can I drive you if we don't have a car?"

His boss sighed. He was getting a headache. "Do I have to think of everything?" he asked. "Call for another car, you fool."

"Right." The driver bit his lip. "We still going after that James Bond Jr., then?"

"Oh, yes," his boss said. "He still has something I want very badly. Perhaps our man at the

Academy will be able to get it for me. But it's better to make certain."

He looked at the wrecked Rolls-Royce, then at the two motorcyclists who'd let young Bond escape. It was so hard to get good crooks these days. He thought for a moment, then took a small wallet-shaped device from his pocket. "And I think I may need some better help than you clowns." He opened the device, which was a small electronic diary. In the bottom left-hand corner were the words SABOTEURS AND CRIMINALS UNITED IN MAYHEM. Switching on the diary, he started to index through the names for the one he wanted. Then he smiled. "Ah!"

The readout lit up: JAWS

This was more like it. . . . The Scumlord chuckled nastily to himself as he read the information he had on file. Jaws was tremendously strong, a bit stupid, but very, very good at getting things done. He'd earned his name because he had steel teeth that could rip metal in half. His fee was a little high, but if this caper came off as he intended, S.C.U.M. would have more money than they'd know what to do with. In that case, Jaws would be a bargain.

The prospect of millions and millions of pounds, dollars, rubles, francs, and any other currency he could think of brought back his good humor. Soon, very soon, James Bond Jr. was going to make Scumlord the richest man in the world!

Chapter Two
Bond Drops In

Warfield Academy is listed in the school guides in England as "exclusive." Most of the parents of the students there take that to mean "expensive," but that is just a part of it. The school is composed of several buildings, almost all of which were built in the nineteenth century by Lord Dover. He had picked a beautiful site, overlooking the water on the south coast of England. The main building had large windows, long corridors, and huge, wood-paneled rooms. Paintings by all of his favorite artists hung in the rooms. Fancy furniture filled the halls.

There was a huge ballroom. The ceiling was almost thirty feet high. Lords and ladies from all over England had been invited to spend weekends at the estate, fishing and shooting in the grounds.

There were several additional buildings—a

gatekeeper's lodge, stables for the many horses he had loved to race, a groundskeeper's cottage. The grounds were large and varied, and Lord Dover had kept two landscapers busy for all of his life.

Then he had died without an heir, and the government took over the estate. All of the paintings and furniture were taken off to fancy museums in London. And the house was turned into Warfield Academy.

Over the years, the place changed. Two wings were built, with dormitories for the male and female students. The ballroom was turned into a gym. The guest bedrooms were stripped of their rich furniture and turned into classrooms. And the whole estate was ringed by a security fence and laser scanners. The high fence made it look more like a prison than a school.

But all of the security wasn't to keep the students in—it was to keep outsiders out.

The students at Warfield Academy weren't there because they were especially bright—even though some really were geniuses. They weren't there because their parents were rich—though many of them were. They were all there because their parents were important people—prime ministers, leaders of industry, brilliant scientists, or top military brains. The one thing that every student at Warfield had in common was that they each might at some time or other be the target of criminals who might kidnap them to use as hostages against their parents.

The students themselves referred to the school as "High Risk High." They were all at risk, constantly. And the high cost of staying here went to cover the sophisticated security system. And, while it was meant to keep intruders out, it also effectively kept the students in. The students had to sign in and out every time they left the grounds. They had to have passes to go anywhere overnight. And these passes were given out only by the headmaster or one of three special teachers—and then only when they were certain there was no unusual risk to the student.

Now, at the start of the new term, students from all over the world had arrived back at Warfield. There was the son of a wealthy raja of India; the oldest daughter of a Texas billionaire; the twins of the prime minister of the new African country of Katawa and many, many others. Almost two hundred in all.

They were gathered in the main hall, facing the stage, with the huge floor-to-ceiling windows on their right. On the stage, the staff of the Academy looked out over the faces of the students. In the center of the stage was a lectern with a microphone. At exactly nine A.M., Mr. Milbanks, the headmaster, walked onto the stage, followed by the gym teacher, Mr. Mitchell.

Mr. Milbanks was neatly dressed in a gray suit, his graying hair brushed back, and his mustache clipped tidily. Everything about him said that he was a neat, clear-thinking person who lived a well-ordered life—and that he expected nothing less from his students. His eyes took in the students. Clearing his throat, he switched on the microphone.

"I want to welcome all of you to Warfield Academy at the start of this new term." He spoke with a clipped, proper English accent. "Some of you are returning to these hallowed halls of learning. For others, this is your first semester."

Then his eyes focused on an empty seat three rows from the front. As always, he had made certain the janitors had put out exactly the right number of seats for the students. He turned to Mitchell, who stood quietly by his side. This teacher also had a neat mustache, but there the similarity between the two men ended. Mitchell was four inches taller and much more muscular. He, too, wore a suit, but he looked very uncomfortable in it. His build showed that he would probably rather be out on the track than indoors, and there was a faint layer of sweat on his rich, dark skin.

"Someone is missing," Mr. Milbanks whispered, covering the microphone with his hand. "You know that I do not tolerate lateness! And *never* on the first day of a new term."

Mitchell nodded thoughtfully. When he spoke, his accent had a trace of a New Orleans drawl to it, betraying his background. "You think that this missing person could be in trouble?" From the way he raised his eyebrows, it was clear he had a pretty good idea just who was missing.

"Believe me," the headmaster said firmly, "if he or she *isn't* in trouble, they soon will be. I will not allow such disregard for the clock. Perhaps you had better call the front gate and find out who has not signed in yet. Then we can—"

A bleep came from Mr. Milbanks's inside pocket. His hand shot toward the small walkie-talkie he kept there, close to his heart. Then a second sound came from outside—an airplane engine.

"What is it?" the headmaster snapped into the walkie-talkie.

"Main gate security," came the answer. "We've got an intruder."

"What sort of intruder?"

"Well, sir . . ." the guard answered. "It looks like a flying car."

"A . . . what?" Mr. Milbanks spluttered.

The sound of the airplane engine was much louder, and the students fidgeted in their chairs. Then one, close to the big windows, jumped to his feet, pointing. "Look at that!"

Outside, there was a flash of light as the car-plane touched down in the parking lot. By the time the dust had settled, the wings and propeller were gone, and the Aston Martin was motoring smoothly into a vacant parking space.

"Totally awesome," said a voice in the crowd.

On the stage, Mitchell raised an eyebrow. "I believe that must be the tardy student, Mr. Milbanks," he said.

As James opened the door of the Aston Martin, he was greeted by two large men wearing Warfield Academy uniforms. If that worried him, he didn't let it show. "I see the service is top-notch around here," he said with a smile. He turned to one of the men and said, "You must be the parking attendant. And you've come to help me with my suitcases, have you? They're in the—"

"Who are you?" the larger of the two asked gruffly. They were not amused.

"Bond," he replied. "James Bond. Junior."

Chapter Three
Welcome to Warfield

James stood stiffly in front of the headmaster's desk, staring at the wall behind Mr. Milbanks's head. The room was like the headmaster—neat and tidy, with everything in its proper place. There were metal filing cabinets for the school records, a big window looking out onto the parking lot, and a large mirror on the wall opposite this window. Mr. Milbanks sat behind a massive oak desk. Aside from a writing set, a blotter, a framed photograph, and two telephones—one a bright red—the desk top was empty. No papers, no rubber bands, nothing.

It was a quarter after nine on James's first day at his new school. He was in trouble already. It was obvious from his crisp white shirt and perfectly knotted tie that this headmaster had a certain way of doing things. He knew Mr. Milbanks wouldn't put up with students who didn't behave the way he wanted. James had run into a lot of headmasters like this in his school days. Mainly because his own thinking was usually a few steps out of line from the perfect students such headmasters seemed to want.

Glaring up at him, the headmaster said: "That was quite an entrance, Master Bond." James said nothing, but looked down at the desk. Mr. Milbanks added: "I will make some allowances, since you are new here. But at Warfield Academy we do not tolerate tardiness. Or—ah—attention-getting behavior. Do I make myself clear?"

"Yes, sir." James's eye fell on the photo on the headmaster's desk. It showed a brown-haired girl, about his age, very pretty, with a cheery grin. James wondered who it could be. And if he'd get a chance to meet her.

"Very few young men and women have the opportunity to study here," Mr. Milbanks continued, unaware of what James was really paying attention to. "You would not wish to ruin your chance, would you?"

"Yes, sir," James said. Catching his mistake, he hastily added: "I mean, no, sir. I very much want to be here at Warfield."

"Good." The headmaster stood up, smiling faintly. "And since you want to be here so much, I will help you. I am confining you to the school grounds for the entire week."

James's face fell. "But, Mr. Milbanks . . ." he

protested weakly. He caught sight of the headmaster's stern face. Then he straightened up. "Yes, sir."

"Good. Keep up that spirit, Bond, and we should get along just fine." He looked down at his desk. "Dismissed."

James wasn't sure if he was expected to salute, or what. He wasn't too impressed with this first meeting. Mr. Milbanks had not even given him the chance to explain his actions. He clearly felt that there could be no excuse for breaking the rules.

James quietly left the office. In the corridor outside, Mr. Mitchell was waiting. More trouble?

"A little rough on you, was he?" the gym teacher asked.

James shrugged.

Mitchell cracked a smile. "If you're anything like your uncle, you probably deserved it. Double-O-Seven is the biggest . . . rule-breaker I know."

James grinned. "I only wish I were more like him. In other ways, I mean." He looked at the teacher with new respect. "You know my uncle, Mr. Mitchell?"

"Yes. I used to work with Double-O-Seven and Felix Leiter. I'm the gym teacher here at Warfield," he said, extending his hand.

James politely shook his hand. It seemed like quite a comedown—trading the action and excitement of the spy world for the quiet boredom of an English school. Most field agents could transfer into training, or desk jobs. Why hadn't Mr. Mitchell?

Mitchell gave him a look, as if he could read James's mind. "You're more like your uncle than you think. And not just because you look like he did at your age. Come on, since this is your first day, I'll show you around. Lessons don't start until tomorrow." He started off, and James fell in behind him. "This is the computer room," the teacher said, gesturing to one door. "We make sure all our equipment here is up to date. Almost all jobs nowadays involve computers. And we have in our classes people who will one day become key figures in industry and the sciences. Over there is the Physics Lab, and the Geography Room. Down that corridor is the gym." He led the way outside. "Playing fields," he said, pointing. "Hope you're good at soccer. We need a new center forward for the team."

"I do my best, Mr. Mitchell."

"That's all we ask," he replied. He pointed to a small building just behind the main part of the school. "That's Mr. Milbanks's house. He stays on the grounds during the term. Most of the teaching staff live in the nearby villages."

"Does that include you?" James asked.

Mr. Mitchell shook his head. "I'm on campus, too. I have a lot of . . . extra duties." *Gym instructors don't usually live on campus,* James thought. *And they don't look after new students very often, either.* There seemed to be depths to this man that weren't normal for a phys ed teacher. After a moment, Mr. Mitchell pointed again. "That building over by the cliffs there houses the diving gear. We give scuba lessons, being so close to the sea."

James grinned. "That sounds like fun."

"It is fun," Mitchell told him, "but don't get the idea you can clown your way through school. You have to know when to follow instructions to the letter." He gave James that odd look again. "And when to disregard them, too."

"I always enjoy learning," James replied, unsure of what he should say. Mr. Mitchell was not giving him much to go on. But if he knew his uncle and had been in the FBI, Mr. Mitchell would be a good person to have on his side. Especially if James ran into more situations like the one he had had on the way to Warfield when those guys had chased him. He still couldn't figure that out.

"Over there is the girls' dorm," the gym teacher said, pointing to the building. He gave James another look. "That's out of bounds to you after nine P.M. Strictly. And no female visitors in your room after that time, either."

James nodded. "I understand."

Mitchell frowned, but said nothing to this. Instead, he led James the other way. "And this is your new home—the boys' dorm. Everyone here shares a room with another student. You know the room number?"

James jingled the key in front of him. He opened the door to the dormitory, but paused before entering. "I couldn't help noticing on my way in that you have quite a good security system here."

The teacher snorted. "Students at Warfield Academy are the sons and daughters of important people. The security system has to be good in order to protect them."

"It seems very efficient," James said.

Mitchell nodded. "Most of the time it is," he agreed. "And if you're confined to the school grounds for the week, you won't be able to get out past them." He thumped James hard on the back and walked off.

How did Mr. Mitchell know about his being grounded already? Had he been listening at the door to the headmaster's office? Or was it the usual punishment for any offense? If it was, he might never get off the school grounds!

He wondered again if Mr. Mitchell was simply what he seemed to be—a teacher. It wasn't that easy to quit the spy game. Maybe . . . maybe he hadn't really quit.

Yeah, right, James thought. *Secret agents teaching soccer and badminton!? I must be crazy.*

He took the stairs three at a time, then looked for his room. When he opened the door, he was amazed at what he saw inside. He simply stopped and stared.

Chapter Four
Hi, IQ

The room was about twenty feet square, with a window opposite the door. It had two sets of identical beds, dressers, desks, and chairs. They were standard for all of the dorm rooms. It was what filled the rest of the room that had surprised James.

On every inch of open space, there were test tubes, flasks, jars of chemicals, electronic machines, wires, and batteries. There were screwdrivers, pliers, wire cutters, and other tools scattered everywhere.

"I thought this was supposed to be a dorm. It looks kind of like Dr. Frankenstein's lab to me," James joked.

The door to the bathroom swung open, and James saw a strange-looking boy inside. "It is the

dorm," the boy said. "But they won't let me do this in the Physics Lab."

James looked at him. He was small, with a mess of blond hair that stuck up on top and flopped down in the front over his forehead. Large, red-rimmed glasses sat on the boy's nose. He wore the school uniform, its tie twisted to one side. Over his clothes he had on a flapping lab coat. It had stains all over it, and even a few burn marks. His shoes were dirty, the laces untied. His hands were hidden inside thick white gloves, and he carried a test tube, which held some silvery liquid that fizzed and spat.

"Why won't they let you do this in the Physics Lab?" James asked.

"I don't know. I guess they don't think it's very safe, for some reason."

James looked at his new roommate. He definitely looked messy, but he probably wasn't too dangerous. "Dr. Jekyll, I presume," James joked.

"Horace Boothroyd, actually," the other boy said, and stuck out a gloved hand. It was the one with the test tube, so he switched it quickly. "But my friends call me IQ."

"IQ?" James shook his hand. "My name's James. James Bond Jr. I'm your new roommate." He looked around. "But you haven't left me much room."

"Oh, I'm sorry," IQ apologized. "I got here early, and there were one or two experiments I wanted to try out."

"I take it you're Warfield's resident genius," James said, staring at all of the equipment.

"Not really," IQ replied. He started to pour the fizzling liquid into a battered saucepan. "I do like to invent things, though. Runs in the family." He looked for a place to put the empty test tube, but there wasn't any space. Finally, he dropped it into his pocket. "My grandfather and your uncle are friends. He's known as Q."

"Q!" James laughed. "I should have known!" Q was the scientist who invented all of the amazing gadgets and weapons his uncle used.

"Of course," IQ added, "there's a lot of things my grandfather isn't allowed to tell me because they're top secret. So I have to figure them out for myself."

James looked at the pan with interest. "So what's your latest brainstorm?"

IQ grinned. "A superconducting liquid."

"A what?"

"Superconducting." IQ smiled. "Let's say you're cooking something like," he fished in his pockets, and pulled something out, "an egg! You have to boil the water, then drop the egg in and wait for three minutes till it's cooked. Now, that seems like a waste of time and energy, because you don't really want to cook the water, right? Just the egg. So," he pointed at the sizzling silver liquid in the pan, "I invented this, which I call Q-rious." He smiled. "Q-rious, *curious.* Get it?"

"Very clever," James told him.

"Yes, I thought so." IQ smiled down at the liquid. "And it is curious. It doesn't heat up itself, you see. It stays cold, and conducts the heat to whatever is in it. It can boil a three-minute egg in just ten seconds." He dropped the egg into the pan. The silvery stuff fizzed and spat even more violently.

"Just the thing when you're in a hurry," James said. IQ was so excited he was practically hopping up and down.

"Not only that," he said, "but the Q-rious itself never heats up. If you spill some while you're cooking, it won't burn you. This could really change the way we cook!"

James looked at the pan. The egg did seem to be boiling. "Can you drink that stuff?" he asked.

"Oh, no!" IQ looked shocked. "It's extremely poisonous!"

"Then isn't there a chance it might poison anything that you cook in it?" James asked.

IQ's face fell. He hadn't thought about that. He was about to say something when they heard a funny sound from the pan. The egg seemed to be ticking. IQ looked puzzled, and they both stared into the pan.

Then, with a loud cracking noise, the egg split open and yolk started to bubble out of it. James and IQ looked down at it again. The egg was bouncing all around like a pinball in the Q-rious.

"I don't want to worry you," James said, "but that egg looks a little hyper to me."

"It's just . . ." IQ began, but the liquid gave one final tremendous burp.

James quickly pushed IQ to the floor. The egg exploded out of the pan and straight through the window, leaving an egg-shaped hole in the glass. Jumping to their feet, they watched the egg soaring off into the distance.

"Congratulations," James said. "You've invented the UFE. Unidentified flying egg."

IQ blinked and looked through the hole in the glass. "Well, at least it gives me a chance to try another of my inventions. I call it glass putty. You see, it's like glass, only you can shape it with your fingers, and . . ."

Chapter Five
Surf's Up

They tried to fix the window with IQ's glass putty, but it kept sticking to their fingers. Finally they patched the broken pane with a piece of cardboard and IQ moved some of his experiments. After James unpacked, IQ took him outside to show him around the grounds. It was a warm day, and as they walked around the Academy they stayed in the shade of the abundant apple trees.

"When's lunch around here?" James asked. "I'm starved."

IQ pulled back the sleeve of his lab coat and looked at his wristwatch. It was a lot larger and thicker than a normal watch. There were several little buttons on the sides, too.

"Interesting," James said.

IQ grinned. "This is one of my greatest inventions," he said proudly.

"I hate to tell you this," James told him seriously, "but they invented wristwatches decades ago."

"Not like this one," IQ promised. "Look." He carefully lined the watch up with one of the trees, and then pressed a button in the side.

With a flash of light, a small, dartlike missile shot out of the watch and rocketed toward the tree above them.

"A built-in rocket launcher," IQ said proudly.

The missile shot through the branches and leaves, and a second later an apple fell from the tree. James caught it and stared at it in open admiration. "Nice shot. IQ, you really are a genius."

While James munched on the apple, IQ led the way into the dining hall. Inside the building, there was a flight of steps leading down to the kitchen, though the dining area was upstairs. Some of the students had already picked up their food, and others were heading downstairs to fill up their metal trays. James picked up a tray from the pile and headed downstairs.

Just ahead of them was a muscular boy with shaggy blond hair. He wore a bright Hawaiian shirt and long shorts, along with hiking boots and thick socks. He set his tray down on the floor, half hanging over the edge of the stairs.

"Gordo!" IQ called out, and the other student looked around. "Meet James Bond, the latest addition to the peanut gallery here at Warfield."

Gordo stuck out his thick hand, and almost

crushed James's when he shook it. "I heard you were on your way here," he said. "My dad works with your uncle—his name is Felix Leiter."

Uncle James's CIA contact! James grinned and shook his head. With all these important people's kids around, there was bound to be some trouble. Good trouble. The kind James could have a blast getting into. And out of. This place was looking more and more interesting.

"Good to meet you," James said.

Gordo shrugged. "Catch ya later," he promised. "I feel a tubular wave coming on!"

"A wave?" Indoors?

"Hang ten!" yelled Gordo, jumping onto his tray. "Surf's up!" His weight carried the tray over the edge of the stairs. Then he threw out his arms, balancing, as the tray shot down the steps. With a neat move of his waist, he spun past two startled-looking students, aiming for a spectacular finish. He almost got more than he wanted, because a young girl stepped right into his path, her eyes on her tray and not on wave-riding maniacs.

"Tracy, look . . ." Gordo started to yell, but it was too late. He shot past her, spinning her around, and sending her tray flying.

James moved quickly, catching the airborne tray, and turned around to present it back to the surprised girl as she regained her balance. "Shaken, not stirred," he told her.

As he looked into her warm, brown eyes, James thought he had met this girl before. She had short brown hair and was wearing an open jacket with a T-shirt under it, and blue jeans.

"Gordo," she yelled over her shoulder. "How many times has my father told you not to surf indoors?"

"Dunno," Gordo called back as he skidded to a halt. "Don't keep count."

Tracy sighed and took her tray from James. "You must be James Bond."

"Let me guess," James said, smiling. "Your father works with my uncle?"

"No," she answered. "I saw your picture in Father's files. You're his latest headache, I understand."

"Oh?" James asked, puzzled.

"I'm Tracy Milbanks," she said, holding out her free hand. "My father's the headmaster." So that was why she looked familiar! She was the girl in the photo on his desk! She smiled. "But don't think for a minute that getting friendly with me will help you with him."

James shook her hand. "Getting friendly with you would be a pleasure," he told her, "no matter who your father is." He meant it—he could tell Tracy was smart and nice, as well as being pretty.

"Oh, brother!" said a second female voice from behind him on the stairs. "What a line!" The girl came around and shot him a filthy look, which changed to one of wide-eyed wonder. "Oh, brother—what a hunk!"

James looked at her. She was short, had blond

hair, and was a little chubby. She wore a purple skirt and top, and carried a large handbag that looked very heavy. She was batting her eyelashes at him through the lenses of thick-rimmed glasses. Her round face broke into a big smile. James put out a hand.

"The name's James," he told her. "James Bond Jr."

Grabbing his hand, she breathed: "Of course it is!" Then she coughed. "Er, I'm Phoebe. Phoebe Farragut."

"Delighted, Phoebe," James said, finally managing to pull his hand free of her strong grip.

"Not half as much as I am," she replied, still staring at him.

James turned back to Tracy. She seemed amused.

"Phoebe and I are roommates," she explained. "Once you get past her . . . enthusiasm, she's really a great person."

"Gee, thanks a lot, Tracy," Phoebe said. "Yes, James, I am a great person."

"I'm sure of that," James agreed. Then someone pushed him aside and burst through the group. James saw a tall, skinny youth with a thin face, sandy hair, and a sneering mouth. His bow tie was neat, his clothing expensive.

"Out of the way," the newcomer said. "This is a hallway, not a meeting room."

James resisted his urge to put this snob in his place. But he'd better not on his first day at Warfield. Especially after already getting in trouble for lateness. "Who is that?" he asked.

"That's Trevor Noseworthy the Fourth," Tracy said, rolling her eyes.

"A real wally," Phoebe added.

"And a world-class dweeb," Gordo finished, joining them.

Tracy looked at James. "He was born into money and snobbery. I guess brains weren't included."

"Well," James said slowly. "He'd better start learning some manners. Or I'll just have to take a hand in improving his education myself."

He collected his food and joined IQ, Gordo, Tracy, and Phoebe upstairs to eat. James noticed that Tracy was friendly with IQ. He wished she'd become that friendly with him. She was certainly James's sort of girl—pretty, bright, funny, and with a mind of her own. She looked in his direction and smiled. James felt his cheeks turn bright red. Did she know he had been staring at her?

You've got other things to worry about! James reminded himself. *Like those motorcyclists who chased you earlier. What was all that about,* James wondered for the tenth time.

Lunch was surprisingly good for school food. While they ate, James learned a lot about his new friends and about Warfield Academy. But the whole time he was eating, James's mind kept wandering back to his escapade that morning. He'd almost been killed. The more he thought about it, the more he wanted to know about his pursuers.

After lunch, James and Gordo collected the trays to return them to the stacks. As they headed across the room, one of the kitchen staff bumped into James. He felt a soft touch, and then the man moved away.

James immediately reached into his pocket.

The keys to the Aston Martin were gone!

"Hey!" James yelled. The man looked around, saw that his theft had been spotted, and took off running down the stairs.

James dropped all but one tray, then threw that onto the top step. Copying what he had seen Gordo do earlier, he surfed it down the steps and onto the lower floor. The fleeing man, seeing James behind him, dived into the kitchen.

"Way cool!" laughed Gordo, skidding to a halt beside James on his own tray. "For an English dude, you hang a mean wave."

"Thanks, but right now I've got to catch that thief," James told him. "He seems to have stolen my car keys."

"Truly, dude?" Gordo asked. But he ran with James into the kitchen. They were just in time to see the man passing through the back doors. They were not in time to see the man carrying the huge bowl of boiled potatoes. Gordo slammed into the man, and the bowl went flying.

James dived between the cooks. He heard the bowl come down, and someone yelling as hot po-

tatoes skidded all over the floor. James hit the back door and sprinted outside.

The thief was just ahead of him, looking over his shoulder as he ran. He paused long enough to push over a garbage can. Then he kicked it at James's feet. James jumped the can and continued the chase.

Gordo shot out of the kitchen moments later, ducking thrown potatoes. "Hey, like, I said I was sorry," he howled, looking back.

The crook had almost made it to the parking lot when James caught up with him. He threw himself at the man's ankles in a tackle, and brought him down. The keys rattled out of the man's hand onto the ground. As James reached for them, the thief leaped to his feet and started running—

—right into Mr. Mitchell. The gym teacher, seeing what was going on, grabbed the man and hauled him off the ground with ease.

"That man tried to steal my car," James said.

"Oh, did he?" Mr. Mitchell looked at the man. "Well, we can't have that, now, can we?" He grinned at the man. "I think we'll let the local police have a word with you. Come on."

"So, what's going on, dude?" Gordo asked when he finally caught up.

James showed him the car keys. "I don't know," James said. "But I plan on finding out."

Chapter Six
Good Sports

Mr. Mitchell stood on the sidelines evaluating his soccer players. He had them practice passing the ball back and forth to one another so he could see how good their aim and speed were.

James passed the ball to Gordo, who stopped it neatly with his foot and then kicked it back. James passed upfield to IQ, who was holding on to his glasses with one hand as he ran along. Waving wildly, IQ dashed at the ball, but fell headlong onto the ground as another player tripped him. IQ's glasses bounced off his nose, and he groped around on the grass hunting for them. The player who had fouled him dropped the glasses in front of his face and IQ glared up.

It was Trevor Noseworthy, and he stared down his thin nose at IQ. "Sorry about that, old chap," he said. "But you really should watch where you're going. You're playing with the big boys now."

James and Gordo ran over and helped IQ to his feet. "You did that intentionally," James said, glaring at Trevor.

"Me?" Trevor tried to look innocent. "You must be joking. I wouldn't waste my time on him." He turned his back and added: "Or on you."

"There goes one bogus guy," Gordo said. "He's in dire need of a chill pill."

James nodded. "I believe you're right. And I think I've got just the right prescription."

Gordo grinned. "All *right*! My man has a plan!"

James nodded and leaned closer to his friends. He explained what he had in mind.

On the other side of school, Tracy and Phoebe had field-hockey practice. Phoebe was bundled up in pads and put in to guard the goal.

"Good," she said. "They can't possibly expect me to do much running around with all this on."

Tracy looked comfortable in the uniform of shorts and top. She smiled at her friend. "Suits you," she joked.

"Still, I probably look ridiculous." Phoebe sighed. "I'm glad James can't see me like this. Do you think he likes me, Tracy?"

"I think he likes any girl," Tracy told her. "If he's anything like his uncle, that is."

"Do *you* like him?" Phoebe asked.

"Me?" Tracy shouldered her hockey stick.

"He's tall, dark, and handsome. He's smart, funny, and kind. Not my type at all." Then she ran off after the ball.

Watching her friend go, Phoebe wondered if she was going to have to fight Tracy to get James's attention. Then she shrugged. She'd get her man. She *always* got what she wanted.

IQ walked over to the bench at the side of the field where Mr. Mitchell had left his clipboard. Penciled in on it were Mr. Mitchell's ideas for a team. IQ was hunched over studying the notes, and he didn't seem to realize that Trevor had sneaked up on him.

Trevor saw IQ bent over the bench, his behind sticking out. "What a shot," he said quietly to himself. "I'd never forgive myself if I passed up a chance like this." He moved quietly to stand behind IQ, and got ready for some serious butt-kicking.

IQ wasn't as out of it as he looked. He could see everything Trevor was doing in the glass face of his watch. Almost in the right place . . . Behind Trevor, James and Gordo were moving into position. . . .

Just as Trevor swung his foot, IQ stepped out of the way. Trevor lost his balance and fell backward. Instead of hitting the ground, however, he slammed into James and Gordo. The two of them were carrying a large cooler filled with water. As

Trevor hit them, they both said "Oops!" very loudly, and tipped the cooler.

Trevor fell on his back on the hard turf. Before he could move, the entire contents of the water cooler soaked him. Spluttering, he wiped the water out of his face and looked up at James and Gordo. The two of them looked away, laughing. They tried not to crack up in Trevor's face, but they couldn't help it. He looked too ridiculous.

"This was your idea, Bond!" he yelled. "I'll get you for this—see if I don't!"

"Look, Trevor," James said, "let's call it even, shall we? Why not just calm down and try and be friends?"

Trevor glared back at him. "It would be beneath my dignity to be friends with riffraff like you," he answered. "And we're even when *I* say we are!" He shook off James's offer of a hand and got to his feet. His cleats squeaking and jersey dripping, he headed toward the changing room. As he left the field, he passed by Mr. Mitchell, who looked at him and shook his head with a smile.

"Noseworthy," he said, "you're supposed to take a shower *after* practice." Then he walked out onto the field. He had a good idea how Trevor had managed to get soaked. He also knew that if anyone deserved a good soak, it was Noseworthy.

"All right, team," he said, calling in the players. "I've got a rough squad together. Leiter, you'll play inside right. Bond, center forward. Singh, inside left." He tried to ignore James and Gordo as they gave each other a high five. Life here at Warfield was getting very interesting. . . .

A black Rolls-Royce was parked off the road just outside the Academy grounds. The rear window was rolled down, and a pair of gloved hands held a battered set of binoculars. The binoculars were focused on the playing field below, on James.

In the back seat of the car, the crime boss sat, scowling. He wore a new hat, since his dog, Scuzzball, had eaten the other. "Enjoy yourself while you still can, young Bond," he said.

Beside the car, in the shade of a tree, stood a huge man. He was at least seven feet tall, and his muscles bulged all over his body. His legs were as thick as tree trunks—he looked like a walking skyscraper. He wore a dark-blue suit that was several sizes too small. Both his ankles and wrists were visible in the gaps. On his coat he wore a red carnation, and his combat boots were so shiny, his monstrous face was reflected in them. But what stood out about him was his face. It wasn't just big and ugly—it was horrible.

Where there should have been lips, gums, and teeth, this monster had a tremendous metal mouth.

Several years before, he had been shot in the mouth while robbing a bank. He had escaped, but to save his life, the doctors had given him a set of metal teeth, and motors for jaw muscles. Now he was back in action, and his metal teeth had given him a new name—and a new weapon.

"Don't worry, Scumlord," he told the man in the car. "I'll take care of him." Bunching up a huge fist, he punched the tree he was standing under. With a loud creaking sound, the tree slowly fell over. Its branches scraped down the side of the Rolls-Royce, leaving bright scratches in the black paint.

Scumlord sighed. Another car ruined. It was one of those days. He stroked his only friend, the white dog that sat in his lap. "I'm impressed by your eagerness to please, Jaws," he told the giant. Jaws, looking red-faced, moved the tree off the car. "However, I am not interested in young Bond himself. I'm interested in the Aston Martin he drove to school."

Jaws pointed to the Rolls-Royce. "But you've already got a nice car," he said.

"I don't want the car, you idiot!" Scumlord yelled. "I want what's *in* it." He smiled. "An experimental E.M.P. generator."

"A what?" Jaws asked.

Scumlord rolled his eyes. "An electromagnetic pulse generator." Since Jaws still looked puzzled —his usual state—Scumlord added: "It produces a beam that can wipe all of the information off a computer disk, or inside a computer memory."

"Is that good?" asked Jaws.

"For S.C.U.M.—yes. For the world—no." Scumlord rubbed his hands together happily. "If I have that machine, I can turn the beam onto any computer I like and destroy everything in its memory."

"I don't get it," Jaws said.

"Well, just think about it, you blockhead!" Scumlord cried. "The police keep all of their records on computer. I could wipe out the criminal record of all the crooks in England. I wonder who'd pay me more—the crooks to do it, or the police not to? All of the national defenses are run by computer. We could knock them all out with the E.M.P. Without computers to run the satellite detection system, dispatch the army and navy, and monitor the attack, England would be open to invasion." He smiled at the thought. "We could even offer to take over the country ourselves as the price for not using the machine. Or we could go to the business district in London and wipe out all of the records there. It would bring industry and banks to a halt. Banks wouldn't know how much anyone had in their accounts!" He laughed evilly. "With the E.M.P. generator, S.C.U.M. could hold England to ransom. We can cause utter chaos in finance, civil defense, law enforcement—any area that we choose! And then we can go on to do the same to any other country in the world! Nobody will be safe from S.C.U.M.—unless they pay us very well indeed. All we need is the E.M.P. machine—and that generator is hidden in the Aston Martin."

Jaws thought about it. "Sounds good. But are you sure it's in the car?"

"Of course I am," Scumlord roared. "S.C.U.M. is spying on top-secret messages that M—the head of the British Secret Service—is sending to James Bond, Double-O-Seven. M doesn't know that we've broken his code, and now know all about the E.M.P. machine."

Jaws nodded. "I'll steal the car tonight."

Scumlord shook his head. "Warfield is protected by the most advanced security system. Somehow, they caught the man that I planted in their kitchens. It would take a small army to get through what they have protecting that school. But you don't have to break in. I have already made my plans. The Aston Martin will be brought out of Warfield and right into our waiting hands by a very special messenger."

"Who's that?" asked Jaws, puzzled.

Scumlord laughed, long and deep. "Why, none other than James Bond Jr. himself . . ."

Chapter Seven
Bond Out of Bounds

Tracy sat at the huge, glowingly clean oak desk in her father's office. She was an only child, and her mother had died years ago. Her father had been busy as a teacher and a headmaster for all of that time, and she'd been moved around a lot before ending up here at Warfield Academy. As a result, she was used to being on her own and doing what she pleased. She was a bit of a tomboy, but not much of a troublemaker. Still, she did have a few habits that her father might not approve of. Like right now. She had picked the lock of his filing cabinet, and sat quietly reading through the file on James. She knew that she wasn't supposed to see it, but if her father didn't know about it, he wouldn't be able to complain. And she wanted to know more about this new student. She'd tried to convince Phoebe that she wasn't curious about him, but she couldn't fool herself. Anyone who flew into school in a car was interesting enough to check up on.

Tracy had learned an awful lot about both the school and other matters from her father's files. Since so many important people's children studied and boarded here, the British Secret Service kept in contact with him. Tracy managed to read many of the files on foreign agents, spies, and crooks that were in England, as well as up-to-date information on anything that might be a problem for the school.

Suddenly the telephone on the desk rang. Tracy looked around—if she didn't answer it, her father might hear it and come in. Then she'd be in big trouble! She picked up the phone, and in her best secretary voice, she said: "Warfield Academy, Mr. Milbanks's office. How may I help you?"

The voice on the other end of the line said: "This is the Post Office in Sawley. We have a parcel here for one of your students. It's marked urgent, but the postman's already left. And we're too shorthanded to be able to send out another man today. I thought the person it's for might want to pick it up himself."

"I'll pass on the message," Tracy said. "Who is the student?"

"It's for a James Bond Jr. From an Uncle James."

Tracy grinned. "I'll be sure he stops by for it. Thank you." She put the phone down. So, he had a parcel in Sawley? Well, this might be her chance to get to know James a little better. She put his file back, then left her father's office. She walked quickly over to the boys' dorm and knocked on the room that James and IQ shared.

James opened the door, and smiled when he saw who it was. "Come in," he told her. "If IQ will just clear some of his junk off a chair, you can even sit down."

"It's not junk," IQ said. "It's science."

"Well, we won't be staying anyway," Tracy replied. "The local post office called. They have an urgent package for you from your uncle."

"That might be important," James said with a frown. Knowing his uncle, the parcel was likely to be something pretty special. "I'd better pick it up right away."

"You can't," IQ said. "Don't you remember? Old Mil—er, the headmaster grounded you for a week. The guards will never let you out."

"That's right." James frowned. Because the faculty and staff were always watching the students, it would be almost impossible to sneak out. Then he smiled at Tracy. "Is there *any* way to get out of here without the security force knowing?"

Tracy pretended to think about it for a minute. Then she grinned. "There might be," she said. "And, for a ride in the Aston Martin, I could show you."

IQ's eyebrows rose. "But that would mean breaking the school rules!" he protested.

"Don't worry about that right now," James told him. "If Uncle James wants me to have that parcel, I've got to get it. No doubt it's much more important than a few rules, don't you think?"

IQ nodded. "I have to agree."

A few minutes later, Tracy led James down the corridor to her father's office. She tapped on the door. "Daddy?" she called. "Are you there?" When there was no answer, she opened the door. "Nobody home. Come on." She led the way into the room.

Outside, Trevor was in the branches of one of the apple trees, watching James and Tracy enter the headmaster's study. "Poking about in the head's office, eh?" he said to himself, smiling. He was balanced on one foot and held on to the tree with one hand as he stretched to see into the window. "I'll just bet that Mr. Milbanks will love to hear about this, Bond. You'll be grounded for the rest of your school life!"

At that moment, Gordo walked by and saw Trevor up in the tree. "Noseworthy never learns," he said to himself. He went over to a close by tap which was connected to the garden sprinkler that watered the trees. Gordo bent down and turned the tap on.

Up in the tree, Trevor was hit right in the face by a stream of water. His grip on the tree branch slipped, and he fell with a cry right on top of the sprinkler.

Gordo grinned. "Awesome. I always knew Trevor was totally wet. Totally!" Then he slipped around the corner of the building before Trevor could see him.

Soaking wet for the second time that day, Trevor started to stomp back inside. On the way, he ran into Mr. Mitchell. The gym teacher looked at him and shook his head sadly.

"Noseworthy, cleanliness is important, but not *that* important. Do you really need all these showers? By the way, it might help if you removed your clothes first."

Trevor just nodded, then squelched on his way. Mr. Mitchell chuckled to himself as he watched Trevor enter the dorm.

Tracy led James to the far wall inside the headmaster's office. There was a large mirror there, with a carved wooden frame. Next to it was a wall lamp. She gripped the lamp and twisted it hard to the left. With a faint whir, the glass in the mirror slid to one side to show an opening in the wall. A spiral staircase led downward.

James looked at Tracy with new respect. He could barely believe what he was seeing.

"Warfield was used by British Military Intelligence during World War Two," she explained. "They built this tunnel in case the Germans ever invaded England. It leads out near the edge of a cliff, where they kept boats hidden. They never did have to use it, and most people forgot it was here. Daddy doesn't have a clue that I know about it. And I'm pretty sure that the security people don't know that it's here."

They stepped through the frame, and Tracy hit a switch on the inside wall. The mirror slid back into place behind them. Tracy reached for a small hole in the wall and pulled out a flashlight, which she clicked on. They could see the steps leading down quite clearly now.

"So, how come you know so much about the secrets of Warfield Academy?" James asked, following her carefully.

"I read a lot," she told him. "You'd be surprised what you find out."

As he entered the school building, still dripping water all over, Trevor spotted Mr. Milbanks. "Sir! Sir!" he called out.

The headmaster turned and stared at him. "Noseworthy, what on earth are you doing?"

"Quickly, sir!" Trevor cried. "Back to your office! This is really urgent!"

"What are you talking about?"

Trevor smiled. "It's Bond, sir. I saw him go into your office and start to look in your files." Better not mention that Tracy was with Bond.

"What?" The headmaster looked furious. "Come along with me, Noseworthy. If this is true, I'll see young Bond is restricted to his room for the rest of the term!" He marched down the corridor to his room and threw open the door.

There was nobody there at all.

Slowly, Mr. Milbanks turned to Trevor. "Noseworthy," he said. "You're dripping on my priceless Persian carpet. There's no sign of anyone in my office but you and I. I trust you have a very good explanation for your behavior." He closed the door behind them very quietly.

Trevor's face had turned completely white.

The steps ended, and a long tunnel stretched out in front of them. James touched the walls. Solid rock. This was some old cave, probably used centuries ago by smugglers. Someone had found it and built the passage up to the study. Clever! Warfield was a special place, all right—and had been for several hundred years.

He and Tracy followed the tunnel until there was daylight ahead of them. Tracy switched off the flashlight and put it into another of the holes in the wall. "For the return trip," she told James.

"Do you do this a lot?" he asked her.

"Only when Daddy grounds me for breaking one of his silly rules. He's awfully fond of rules. Or when there are important packages to pick up." She led the way out of the cave and through a thick mass of bushes.

"These hide it from the road," Tracy explained. "If you didn't know the cave was here, you would never be able to find it."

James was impressed, but he also realized that if anyone ever discovered this cave was here, some villains might use it to sneak into the school. Should he report it, and cover a breach in the security? Or keep quiet, and have a secret way in and out of the school if the need should arise? Well, no need to decide right away. First he'd make sure that they'd really escaped unnoticed.

They were standing by the road that led to Sawley. In the distance, they could see the fences and the security area that surrounded the school. They had managed to dodge the security system!

"Tracy, you're incredible," he told her.

"I know," she said calmly.

At that moment, they saw the Aston Martin coming down the road toward them. They ran out of the cave and waved it down. For a second, it looked as if the car wouldn't stop. Then, in a screech of brakes, it came to a halt just a few feet ahead of them.

IQ got out of the driver's seat, looking a little confused. He pushed his glasses back onto his nose. "You were right, James," he said. "I had no trouble getting past the main gate."

"Thanks for bringing it, IQ," James said, getting into the driver's seat. Tracy climbed into the back seat, and IQ took the passenger side.

"That's okay," IQ replied. "I've never driven a car before, and I always wanted to have a go." He smiled at James. "It really is very interesting, isn't it? Mind you, I have got a couple of ideas that might get it to work better."

James gave him a look. "You've never driven a car before?"

IQ shook his head. "That's why I took so long," he explained. "I had to figure out how it worked first."

James sighed. "Now you tell me!" Shifting into gear, he pointed the car's nose in the direction of Sawley and roared off.

Chapter Eight
Missing: One Aston Martin

Sawley was a small village. It had a few shops, a number of houses and cottages with flower-filled gardens, one bank, and the post office. This was in an old, stone-faced house, and the red sign hung outside was the only way of knowing it was the village post office. There were just a couple of other cars around when the silver Aston Martin came into town. Of course, they were all parked close to the post office, so James was forced to park down a small side street.

"Here already?" Tracy asked. She had been enjoying the ride. It really was an amazing car.

"I'm afraid so," James said. "I'll only be a minute. Are you two coming, or staying here?"

"I've seen the place," Tracy told him. "I'll wait here."

"I'll come along," IQ said. "I need some fresh batteries from the shop next door."

As soon as James and IQ had left, Tracy started poking around. "Right. Now let's take a look at this terrific car. . . ." She leaned forward to look over the front seats. "There are supposed to be all kinds of gadgets in it, and—"

In the rearview mirror, she saw someone coming down the tiny street toward the car. He was gigantic, wearing a too-small dark-blue suit, and flashing a sharklike smile.

"What a monster!" she said to herself. As he got nearer and she could make out his face, she began to tremble. "I've never seen someone so gross." In fact, he was terrifying looking.

He was coming straight for the car. Tracy thought about sounding the horn to warn James, but there was no time. Just to be on the safe side, she slid down between the front seats and hid in the back.

Jaws stopped by the side of the Aston Martin and smiled his big, metal grin. Perfect! The car was empty, and the Bond kid was in the post office. He tried the driver's door, and it was unlocked. He wedged himself into the seat, and then felt around under the steering wheel until he found the ignition wires. He ripped the wires out of their casing and bit through them. He had the car started in a few seconds. After all, he'd been hotwiring cars since he was a boy.

* * *

The postal clerk shook his head. "Sorry, Mister Bond," he said. "There isn't any parcel here for you at all. I don't know who could have called the school to say there was. Must be a prank."

"Thanks for looking, anyway," James told him.

"I don't get it," IQ said, puzzled. "Why would anyone play a joke on you like this? It doesn't make sense."

"It would if it wasn't a joke," James replied. "Somebody wanted to get me out of Warfield."

"But who would do that?"

James shook his head. "I don't know. But someone tried to stop me getting to the Academy this morning. Then that cook tried to steal my car. This package thing must be linked to it. But—"

He broke off as they heard the distinctive purr of the Aston Martin's engine. James and IQ looked at each other, then shot outside. They were just in time to see the Aston Martin roar past them, some huge man at the wheel.

"But I've still got the keys," James said.

"But somebody else has the car!" IQ replied.

James ran to the corner where he had parked and slammed his fist against a lamppost. "Worse than that," he told his friend. "They also have Tracy! There's no sign of her here!"

"Fantastic," IQ said, watching the now-empty road. "So what do we do next?"

James looked grim. "It's time to call in reinforcements."

* * *

Fifteen minutes later, a van shot down the quiet main street of Sawley. On the side doors were the words WARFIELD ACADEMY and under them was the school crest. It braked in front of the post office, and Gordo Leiter waved at James and IQ from the driver's seat.

"Thanks for coming, Gordo," James said as Gordo slid out of the driver's seat into the back of the van. Then James noticed who was in the passenger seat. "Phoebe! What are you doing here?"

"Tracy's my best friend," she replied. "If she's in trouble, I want to help."

"But this could be dangerous," James told her. "You'd be safer if you stayed here."

"Huh!" Phoebe said, tossing her head. "And what kind of a friend would I be if I didn't do my best to save Tracy?"

James smiled. "You've got a good heart, Phoebe."

Phoebe beamed at him.

Gordo made room for IQ to join him in the back, and then called out: "Let's put the pedal to the metal. To the max!"

As James set the van screeching in the direction that the Aston Martin had disappeared, he asked Gordo: "Did you have much trouble borrowing the van?"

"Nope," Gordo said.

"We didn't ask," Phoebe added. James said nothing, but raised his eyebrows questioningly.

Gordo wiggled his fingers in the air. "I . . . found the keys. They were already in the van."

IQ picked up a box of electronic parts from the floor. "Did you get what I asked for?"

Gordo looked at the box and shook his head. "I'm totally hopeless with technology. I had no idea of what that gizmo you wanted looked like, so I just brought everything from your room that wasn't nailed to the floor."

"Egg timer," IQ muttered, sorting through the box and identifying his inventions. "Electronic bottle opener. Remote control for the TV. Ah!" He pulled out a small device about six inches long, three wide, and one deep. There were several small control knobs on it, a few buttons, and a tiny TV screen. "Tracking device!"

"Most excellent," Gordo said. "What's it do?"

"Every car issued to an agent in the British Secret Service has a built-in homing signal," IQ explained. "Grandfather told me that once. Now, all I have to do is to work out what the right one is . . ."

"And we can track down the Aston Martin," James finished for him.

IQ had the device warmed up, and the screen suddenly lit up in a ghostly green color. With a loud *bleep*!, a small white point began flashing on and off. "Not only can I track it," he added. "I can also send a signal that will take over all of the car's electronics."

"And what would that do?" Phoebe asked.

"It means I can start or stop the Aston Martin by remote control. Or make it change gears and speed up."

Phoebe gave a big grin. "Then you're going to turn its engine off, so we can catch up to it?"

"We can't chance it," IQ told her. "We can only use these controls when we have the car in sight. Otherwise, we can't be certain what might happen if I turned off the engine. The Aston Martin might skid out of control into other traffic, or even crash. We want Tracy back safely. When we see the car, we can use my little gizmo safely."

Phoebe made a face. "So what next?"

"The car is only about ten miles ahead of us," IQ said. "We're going faster than it is. We should catch up with it very soon."

"And then," promised James with quiet determination, "whoever kidnapped Tracy is going to be in major trouble!"

Chapter Nine
On Wings of S.C.U.M.

The Aston Martin sped down the narrow country lanes, then slowed down as it came up behind a large moving van. Jaws, at the wheel of the car, sounded the horn.

But the van didn't get out of the way. Instead, the back of the moving van started to come down. Two men in the back lowered the door until it almost touched the road. Both men were dressed alike, in dark clothing that had the letters "S.C.U.M." on the chest.

As soon as the door was down, Jaws smiled, his metal fangs shining in the sunlight. Then he put his foot on the gas pedal. The Aston Martin hit the door and then shot up it, past the two men and into the back of the van. Jaws slammed on the brakes, stopping the car just short of the cab. The two men then raised the door again; the car had completely vanished from the road.

But not from the screen of IQ's tracking device.

The Warfield Academy van came down the road. James had expected to see his uncle's car right ahead of them, but there was just a slow-moving furniture truck.

"Maybe the car's right in front of the truck?" Phoebe said. "Then we wouldn't see it."

"No," IQ told her. "The homing signal is coming from *inside* the truck."

"Very clever," James said with a smile. "They've planned this well, just in case we could somehow follow them. Too bad they don't know about the homing signal."

"Maybe they do, dude," Gordo said. "This could be a trap, you know?"

"What do we do now?" asked IQ. "There's not much point in using my remote control to stop the Aston Martin—it's already stopped! But the truck carrying it won't be affected by my invention. It's not a secret service vehicle. It's not equipped with the proper remote sensory device to react to our signal."

"Huh? What's that mean?" Gordo asked.

"It means we stay well back, and follow the truck," James decided. "There's more than one man involved in this, clearly. Let's look for a chance to sneak in. They have to stop sooner or later."

"And if it is a trap?" IQ asked.

James grinned. "Then I'll go in and spring it. You three will be my backup."

IQ nodded. "I thought you'd say something like that." He took his wristwatch off and gave it to James. "In that case, you might need this."

James glanced down at it as he followed the moving van. "This is your greatest invention," he said, touched by IQ's gift. He knew how much the watch meant to his friend.

IQ waved his hand in the air. "I think you'll have more use for it than I will." He strapped it onto James's wrist. "Now, this button launches the rockets. There's just two of them. And this button next to it operates a tiny buzz saw."

"I don't think I'll be cutting down trees in that van," James joked.

"It might come in handy if Tracy's tied up," IQ said.

"Ah!" James grinned. "James cuts the bonds!"

"James! Cut the chatter!" Phoebe said, pointing. "The moving van's turning off the road!"

James stopped the Warfield van, and they watched their target. It had left the main road and was going through an open gate in a wire fence. Beyond this was a large open field with a few old, abandoned buildings. On the fence was a sign: MINISTRY OF DEFENSE/SAWLEY FIELD—KEEP OUT.

They watched as the van drove over to one of the buildings and parked. But nobody got out of the van. It looked as if this was the end of the line.

"Come on," James said, turning off the engine. "Let's get a closer look."

The other three followed him. Beside the road, a ditch ran all around the fence. It was muddy and overgrown with weeds, but he led them straight to it.

"Yuck!" Phoebe said. "You expect me to walk through *that*?"

"No choice, Phoebe. We've got to stay out of sight," James told her. "A little mud never hurt anyone. Besides, these people have already tried to kill me once today. If they see us, they'll probably open fire."

At his last words, Phoebe dived right into the mud, with IQ right behind her. James looked at them with a smile. "Well, not that far out of sight," he told them. "Just keep low, okay?"

"Now you tell me," Phoebe muttered disgustedly. She had muddied her best jeans for nothing. And in front of James, too.

James led the way to the gate. About twenty feet away, they could see a small mound in the grass, with concrete entrances to a dark passageway. Gordo grinned.

"Cool, man!" he said. "This looks like something from an old war movie!"

"That's because this *was* used during the Second World War," James replied. "It was one of the bases that airplanes were launched from during the Battle of Britain. That's an old air-raid shelter, and the buildings where the truck is parked was the old HQ."

"So why are the bad guys here?" Gordo asked.

"Well, I don't think they're filming a movie," James replied. He pointed to the landing field. "And that strip doesn't look as run-down as the rest of this place." He frowned. "It looks like this airfield isn't as abandoned as it's supposed to be."

Gordo did a doubletake. "You think these creepazoids aim to catch a flight to freedom?"

"It does look likely," James said. "Come on." He led them in a fast, low run to the shelter. They ducked into the doorway to keep hidden.

Phoebe made a face. "Yuck! Spiders!" She started brushing at the webs that had been made, and then saw something. "James, look!" She pointed into the air.

Coming in low for a landing was a large aircraft. It had a very fat body and large wings. Instead of the usual airline logos on the plane, there was just a peculiar symbol. James recognized it instantly.

"A S.C.U.M. cargo jet!" he said softly.

"S.C.U.M.?" Phoebe asked. "What's that?"

"It's an organization of diabolical people that will do anything they can to destroy all existing forms of government, banking, and industry so that they can take over themselves," James told her.

"You mean like 'today Sawley, tomorrow the world' types?" IQ asked.

"You've got the idea," James said. "Whenever they're around, it means serious trouble."

"Megabummer," Gordo said. "So—what next, dudes?"

James watched the plane as it touched down, braked, then began to taxi toward the waiting moving van. Tracy and the Aston Martin were going to be loaded onto the plane. This whole operation had been planned very carefully—but why? None of it made any sense at all. He knew all about S.C.U.M. from his uncle. They were full of evil ideas and nasty plots to get what they were after. But why were they here, and what did they have in mind by attacking a group of students and stealing his car?

They had gone to a great deal of trouble, so they must be after something really big. He'd just have to play this one out. Hopefully, it would start to make sense to him sooner, rather than later.

Still, it was quite clear that the Aston Martin was going to be loaded onto the plane. If there was any chance of getting either it or Tracy back, they had to act as quickly as possible.

"IQ," he asked, "do you have any of that superconducting liquid Q-rious left?"

IQ reached inside his lab coat and pulled out a test tube of the silvery stuff. "You have an idea?" he asked.

James grinned. "What we need right now is a good diversion."

Chapter Ten
Tracy in Trouble

As the airplane came to a halt, a door in its side opened. In the entrance stood Scumlord. For the first time in ages, he had a large smile on his face. Scuzzball peered out from between his master's legs and growled as Jaws walked over from the moving van. Jaws growled back, showing his metal teeth, and the terrified dog scampered off into the depths of the plane.

"Quickly, you idiot," Scumlord snapped. "Load the car onto the plane."

"But I thought you said you didn't want the car," Jaws said. "Just that thingy in it."

"I *don't* want the car." Scumlord gritted his teeth. Did he have to think for everyone? "But we have to take it apart to look for the E.M.P. device." Scumlord knew that Jaws was strong and fierce, but he wished that his henchman had a few brains to go along with all his muscles.

Jaws grinned and bit at the air. "I can take the car apart real fast right now."

"And if anyone sees us on this closed airfield, they'll call the police," Scumlord answered. "Besides which, there might be a chance that young Bond could have followed you here. I want to be gone before there's any trouble. Now, load the car!"

"All right," Jaws agreed. "But only if I get to take it apart!"

"When we're safely back at base," Scumlord promised him, "you can do whatever you want. You can eat the thing if you want to."

The driver of the moving van was watching Jaws and Scumlord talking. James grabbed his chance and hid behind the front of the van. Quietly, he opened the hood and twisted open the oil cap. He then poured the whole test tube of the silvery liquid into the manifold. *If this works as well on engines as it does on eggs,* he thought, *we'll be in for a real fireworks show.* Then he closed the cap and hood again, before slipping off behind the building.

He watched as Jaws came back over to the van and spoke to the driver. The two of them got into the cab, and the driver started the van's engine.

There was a sudden explosion, and the hood flew up. It hit the windshield, shattering it. Thick black smoke billowed from the engine and started

to fill the cab. The driver slammed on the brakes, and he and Jaws jumped out, coughing. The smoke blinded them.

"What happened?" Jaws asked between loud coughs.

"I don't know," the driver said, coughing and sneezing. "It must have overheated. I'll take a look under the hood."

While the two men were trying to see what had gone wrong, James moved. Hidden from the plane and Jaws by the smoke, he made it to the back of the van. There was a small door set in the loading ramp, and it was unlocked. He jumped inside the van and closed the door behind him. Then he looked around.

There was no sign of the other man who had helped the driver load the car. Nor was there any sign of Tracy. But the Aston Martin stood in the center of the space. James opened the door and peered in. It was empty.

"Tracy?" he called out quietly. "Tracy, can you hear me?"

There was a bang from the trunk, and then another. Pulling the keys from his pocket, James unlocked it and opened it up.

Tracy sat up in the tiny space. Her hair was a mess, and there was a smudge of dirt on her nose. But she seemed to be unharmed.

"Really, Tracy, there's plenty of room for you up front," James told her. "Are you okay?"

"Oh, yes," she said, her eyes blazing. "I just

love spending hours locked in a car's trunk. What kept you? And where am I?"

"Inside a moving van," James told her. "The Aston Martin was stolen by a thug named Jaws."

"Jaws," Tracy said. "When I saw him heading toward the car, I pulled down the rear seat and hid in the trunk. But I couldn't get out again."

"Well," James replied, "I don't think the people who designed the car felt there was a need to open the trunk from the inside."

"I can tell. They didn't even put a TV and refrigerator in there. But now what do we do about—Jaws!"

James frowned. "Avoid him, I hope."

"No!" All the blood had rushed from Tracy's face as she pointed over James's shoulder. "Jaws!"

James spun round. In the doorway stood the hulking, shadowy figure of the S.C.U.M. agent. The huge man smiled, and his metal teeth sparkled.

"It's dinnertime," he said, stepping into the van. "And you're dinner!"

Chapter Eleven
Takeoff!

James looked around quickly. There was no way out except the door—which was behind Jaws. "I'm afraid we can't stay," he said. "We've got lots of homework to do."

Jaws smiled wickedly. "Sorry, Bond—you've just booked a one-way flight on S.C.U.M. airlines."

"I think I'll give it a miss," James told him.

Jaws jumped at them, but James and Tracy ducked under his arms and ran for the door. Outside, the driver and the other man had laser guns in their hands, pointed right at the truck.

"Now what?" Tracy asked. She looked very pale. This wasn't what she'd expected from a ride in James's car! She'd been hoping for a little fun—even a little romance—not a fight for her life.

"Run for it," James replied. He nodded toward the front of the van, past the Aston Martin.

Jaws charged at them again. James picked up a crowbar that was near the door and held it like a club in his hands. Jaws just smiled and jumped at him. James swung the bar, but Jaws grabbed it. Opening his mouth, he bit down with his metal teeth—and the crowbar clattered to the floor in two pieces. James could see the marks of the teeth in the metal. If Jaws bit him or Tracy, he could take off an arm or a leg in one chomp! James gave up on fighting Jaws and tried to dodge away again and join Tracy. She'd managed to reach the front of the Aston Martin.

"There's another door here into the cab, James!" she called.

Jaws realized that she was getting away. With a growl, he turned away from James. Then he *picked up* the back of the Aston Martin—and shoved it forward.

Tracy jumped out of the way just in time. The car slammed into the door where she had been standing. The force of the blow broke the door completely. Just through it, she could see the cab of the van—and the keys in the ignition! If she could get the van started, they could at least get away from the gunmen outside, and the waiting plane.

James jumped onto Jaws's back, hoping to knock him over. He grabbed the giant's arm and tried to wrestle him down. But Jaws didn't even seem to notice the attack. Instead, he reached back and hit James, knocking him to the floor.

James shook his head, trying to stumble back to his feet. His face burned as if it were on fire where Jaws had smacked him. He hadn't expected this to be easy, but now he knew that there was a strong chance Jaws would kill him.

Meanwhile, Tracy jumped up onto the hood of the Aston Martin, ready to dive forward through the doorway. Jaws saw what she was doing and kicked the back of the car. It hit the side of the van and bounced up and down. Tracy screamed and lost her balance, falling backward—right into Jaws's waiting arms.

"Got you!" He laughed, and Tracy shook with terror at the sight of his razor-sharp metal teeth, so close to her. She struggled to get free, but he was much too strong for her.

"Let her go!" James yelled, and ran at Jaws.

For a big man, Jaws could move fast. He twisted around, and his free hand shot out. He grabbed James and lifted him right off the floor. He looked around, and saw the open trunk of the Aston Martin. As James tried to karate-chop Jaws on the neck, Jaws threw him into the trunk. Before James could move, Jaws dropped Tracy right on top of him and slammed the trunk shut.

Grinning, he rubbed his hands together. "Next stop, S.C.U.M. HQ," he roared. "If you want anything, just scream." Then, laughing at his own joke, he climbed into the driver's seat of the Aston Martin. Revving the engine very loudly, he honked the horn for the two gunmen outside to lower the ramp of the van. He backed the car down to the ground and then, tires squealing, started off toward the waiting S.C.U.M. plane.

Still hidden in the doorway to the bomb shelter, IQ, Gordo, and Phoebe watched the car driving across the runway.

"Now what?" Phoebe asked, worried. "There's no sign of James or Tracy at all."

"Beats me," Gordo said. "This is majorly uncool."

"And it's not too good, either," IQ agreed. "It looks like they've both been captured."

"Then it's up to us to save them," Phoebe said. "They're our friends. There must be *something* we can do."

"No way we can go charging in there," Gordo said. "Those goons have got guns. This is one gnarly situation, compadres."

"Totally." Phoebe sighed.

Annoyed with the delays, Scumlord watched the Aston Martin driving toward the plane. He nodded to another of his men, who went to a small control panel near the back of the plane. The body of the aircraft was hollow and very large. Near the nose was the control cabin. A small door separated the cargo section from the first-class cabin where Scumlord and his men would sit for the flight.

The henchman at the back of the plane flipped

a switch. A ramp opened up that led into the cargo space. Jaws raced the car up the ramp and into the body of the plane. The man at the ramp then touched the switch to close the plane up again with the car safely inside.

Jaws jumped out of the Aston Martin and walked over to join Scumlord at the door to the passenger section. He smiled down at his boss.

"I got that young Bond and some girl locked inside the trunk of the car, Scumlord."

"Good." Scumlord thought for a moment. "She must be from that school—which means she's somebody important's daughter. They may pay a lot of money to get her back."

"And what if they won't pay?" asked Jaws.

"Then they won't get her back." Scumlord smiled evilly. "Except in tiny little pieces."

"And the Bond kid?" Jaws asked.

"He can tell us where the E.M.P. device is hidden in the car. And if he doesn't, we'll see how well he flies without his car-plane—or a parachute." He laughed just thinking about it, and Jaws joined in. It would serve that little punk right for making his job so difficult.

Inside the trunk of the car, James and Tracy managed to untangle themselves. James could barely see in the darkness.

James's eyes adjusted and he looked at Tracy, and saw how scared she seemed to be. But she was fighting to control it. She was some girl!

"What do you think is going on?" she asked, making an effort to keep her voice calm.

"We've been loaded onto the S.C.U.M. jet," James replied. He gave her a small smile. "Normally, I wouldn't mind spending time with you, Tracy. But right now, we'd better concentrate on getting out of here."

She gave him a smile back. "If we get back to Warfield safely," she said, "I guess I'll let you hang out with me."

"We'll get back," he promised her.

"That, I believe. But how do you plan on getting us out of here?" she asked.

"That part I haven't quite worked out," he admitted. He tried to push open the trunk, but it stayed firmly locked. Then he tried pushing on the back seat, but it wouldn't move either.

"I tried that last time," Tracy said. Her voice was shaky. "It didn't work. We're stuck in here—until they come for us." James wished he could think of something to say to cheer her up, but his mind was a blank. She was right. They were stuck.

In the cabin of the S.C.U.M. jet, the pilot turned to look over his shoulder. Jaws was just squeezing through the doorway from the cargo bay. "All set for takeoff?" the pilot asked.

Scumlord looked around from his seat. "Are our guests safely on board?" he asked.

Jaws laughed. "Yes, boss. They're nice and cozy in their . . . cabin."

"Excellent," Scumlord said, smiling. "Very well, pilot—let's be on our way."

The pilot nodded. All of the pre-flight checks were finished. He started the plane moving down the runway.

"Next stop—S.C.U.M. headquarters," Scumlord said. He settled back in his chair and started to scratch Scuzzball behind the ears. "Now that I have my hands on the pulse generator," Scumlord told Jaws, "we can begin to blackmail every business in England! They'll only be able to keep their records if I say they can. They won't even be able to open without my permission. They'll have to pay me just to turn on the lights. Soon we will be very, very rich. And England will be very, very poor!" He laughed as he thought about his master scheme. Soon, S.C.U.M. would be running the entire country.

"Ultradowner," said Gordo as he, Phoebe, and IQ watched the cargo plane take off. It rose into the air and was quickly lost in the clouds.

"Right," agreed Phoebe. "It looks like James and Tracy are in serious trouble."

IQ sighed. "I do hope that James remembers I gave him my watch."

Phoebe stared at him. "The last thing James is gonna need to know right now is the time."

"No," IQ said, shaking his head. "I don't want him to look at time. I want him to look at the watch."

Phoebe looked at Gordo. "Do you have any idea what he's talking about?"

"No way. I wish we had an IQ-to-English dictionary."

Phoebe stared at the moving van on the runway. "Well, I think we'd better check out the van."

IQ looked nervously at the waiting van. "But suppose there are some of those armed men still with the van? We could get shot!"

"James and Tracy might really need our help," Phoebe said.

"Right," Gordo agreed. "Besides, we were supposed to be James's backups, remember? He's probably waiting for us to jump in and save him."

IQ nodded slowly. "But what can we do against guns, Gordo?"

Gordo slapped him on the back. "I don't know," he said. "You're the real live genius."

That didn't seem to encourage IQ. "Well, this is one genius who'd like to *stay* live," he sighed.

"Come on, IQ," Phoebe said. "You must have some way of getting them out of there. You're the smartest person I know."

IQ blushed. He thought he had a plan. "Well maybe if we . . ."

Chapter Twelve
Time to Go

Trevor Noseworthy was finally in some dry clothes. He was also in a very bad mood. That Bond fellow had made him look like a fool again. But nobody could beat a Noseworthy. It was just a matter of time until he would be able to get back at Bond. Right now, he was heading quietly down the corridor toward the room James and IQ shared. He was sure that Bond would be doing *something* that could be reported to Mr. Milbanks.

There was a noise from around the corner, and Trevor stopped still. Maybe it was Bond! Then he heard a voice; it wasn't Bond at all. It was Mr. Mitchell.

But what was Mr. Mitchell doing in the boys' dorm at this time of the afternoon? Puzzled, Trevor listened carefully. He realized that the gym teacher was talking on the telephone.

"No, sir," Mitchell was saying. "I've checked his room, but James isn't there. Nor is IQ. And something tells me that Tracy is gone as well." He paused, and then went on. "I know they were supposed to stay in school, sir. But it seems that Bond Jr. is a bit too much like his uncle. No, I don't know how they got out—but they did." Another pause, and: "Yes, sir, I *know* there's trouble. But I don't know where any of them could be. All I can do is to start a search and hope we find them."

There was the sound of the phone being hung up. Trevor held his breath as Mr. Mitchell left in the opposite direction. He was safe!

Bond had disobeyed Mr. Milbanks! He'd not only left the school grounds after being confined there for the week—he'd even taken the headmaster's daughter with him! This was even better than Trevor had expected. Snickering, Trevor ran off to look for the headmaster. This was going to be a very good afternoon. . . .

James wriggled around in the trunk of the Aston Martin. He felt his elbow dig into Tracy's ribs, and she gave a yell.

"Sorry about that," James told her. "It's hard to do anything in here without bumping you somehow."

"Then stay still," she said, rubbing her ribs. "That hurt. How long have we been in here anyway?"

"Time," James whispered, a big grin on his face. "That's the answer!"

"It is?" Tracy sounded lost. "And what was the question?"

"The question is *how do we get out of here*?" James started to wriggle again. Tracy gave another squeal. "Sorry," he told her. "I promise, we'll have more room in a minute."

"That's three bruises I owe you now," she told him. "What are you doing?"

He pointed to the watch. "This is one of IQ's greatest inventions. With its help, we'll be out of here in a second."

"Oh, yeah?" Tracy asked. "What is it? A time bomb?" James had to admire her spunk if she could make puns in a situation like this.

"Not quite," James said. "But you've heard the old saying about time flying. Well, this one really does fly. Just close your eyes and plug up your ears. It's going to get a bit noisy in here."

James aimed the watch carefully at the trunk's lock. He hesitated. What if it didn't work? What if it backfired and blew up the entire car? But he didn't have any choice. IQ's invention was their only chance of escaping.

James closed his eyes and pressed the rocket launch button. There was a small roar, and the tiny missile flashed across the few inches from the watch to the lock. Then it exploded loudly, filling the trunk with smoke.

Coughing and wiping his teary eyes, James

kicked both feet into the lid of the trunk. With the lock now shattered, the trunk sprang open.

James jumped out, still coughing, and reached back to help Tracy. She climbed out and looked around the plane. Finally, she could talk again.

"This isn't what I'd call a whole lot better," she said. "We're out of the trunk, but we're still on a S.C.U.M. plane." She looked out of the nearest window. "And a long way from the ground."

"Then I think it's time we bailed out," James told her. He took the keys to the Aston Martin from his pocket and grinned. "Fancy a ride?"

Tracy paled. She clearly thought he'd lost his mind. "James!" she cried. "We're thousands of feet in the sky. We can't just drive out of here!"

"The Aston Martin has flying adaptations, remember?" He held the passenger door open for her.

Tracy smiled. "That's right!" She got in. "Air Bond to the rescue."

James went around to the driver's seat. "You can copilot on all my flights," he said. Then he started the Aston Martin's engine. In the big, empty cargo bay, the noise of the motor was deafening. But James didn't have time to worry about being quiet.

Inside the passenger area, Scumlord sat talking as usual about his plans for the future. He never got tired of talking about all the different kinds of mayhem he could cause. "We'll begin with the

Bank of England," he said. "That's where all the gold is kept. I'm sure they'll pay me not to wipe out all of their records. Perhaps I'll demand another title, such as duke. Maybe even . . . king! After all, I'm already a Scum*lord*."

"That's really smart," Jaws said.

"Of course it is," Scumlord agreed. "In fact—" He stopped talking as they heard a loud sound from the cargo bay. "What was that?"

"It sounded like a car engine," Jaws said helpfully.

"Well, don't just sit there!" his boss yelled. "It must be that Bond kid! Go and check up on him! And if he's up to anything—kill him!"

James opened the secret panel in the Aston Martin by the gear stick. "Watch this," he told Tracy. Then he pressed the switch for flight conversion.

Nothing happened.

A red light came on under the switch.

"Is that it?" Tracy asked. "A red light?"

James looked under the dashboard. There were wires hanging loose underneath it. "Great!" he said. "Jaws must have cut through the wires when he stole the car. Oh well, I'll have to try an alternate plan of escape."

"James." Tracy pointed. "I think you'd better set that plan in motion."

Jaws was coming through the door from the passenger area. When he saw that James and

Tracy were free, he roared in anger. His huge metal teeth clashed together noisily as he bounded down the floor toward them.

"Well," Tracy said quietly, "shall we surrender now, or wait until he starts biting?"

Chapter Thirteen
Jaws Wars

James looked around the cargo bay. There was nothing he could use as a weapon. And he couldn't possibly beat Jaws in hand-to-hand combat. He was good at karate and other martial arts, but trying that on Jaws would be like trying to stop a tidal wave with a spoon. Taking on Jaws in hand-to-hand combat would be instant death. Or at the very least, dismemberment.

As Jaws came closer, James realized that he and Tracy did have one weapon—they were sitting in it! There was no telling how many of the built-in tricks Jaws had destroyed when he bit through the wires, but the engine was working perfectly.

"Hang on, Tracy!" James yelled, and then put the Aston Martin in reverse.

Tracy screamed as the car shot backward—

right toward the tail of the plane and the loading doors. Would they stay closed if the car hit them? "James!" she yelled, pointing over her shoulder.

"Don't worry, Tracy," he said, slamming on the brakes inches from the doors. "I'm not *that* crazy. I just needed a little more room." With a smile, he put the car into first gear and then shot right at Jaws.

The huge thug stopped dead, and his terrible jaw went slack as he saw the car rocketing toward him. He was tough, but the speeding car hit him by surprise and knocked him off balance. With a yell of panic, he dived back into the passenger area of the plane—and fell straight onto the pilot.

The pilot gave a pained howl as he crashed forward—onto the flight instruments. The plane lurched sickeningly and went into a wild nosedive.

Gordo, IQ, and Phoebe had crept very quietly toward the moving van. There were two S.C.U.M. men left with it, waiting for fresh orders from their boss. Both of them held laser guns.

Gordo grinned at IQ. "So what do we do now?"

IQ looked around nervously. "Phoebe," he whispered. "Do you have a mirror in your bag?"

"You look fine," Phoebe said. "Besides, I don't think this is exactly a good time to worry about your appearance."

"Trust me Phoebe, I need another mirror." IQ pulled two mirrors from his pocket. He handed one to Gordo. "Okay, this is the plan," he whispered. "Now, I'll go around . . ." Then, taking a deep breath and screwing up all of his courage, IQ stepped around the front of the van.

"Er—hi, guys," he said, waving his empty hand. "Excuse me," he said to the taller man. "But your fly is open."

Both men looked down. "Thanks," the taller one said. "It's—" Then he realized what he was doing. "Hey!" he yelled, bringing up his gun. "What are you doing?"

"Looking for a friend of mine," IQ told the men. Both guns were pointed right at him now. He better have worked this out right. Phoebe and Gordo were quietly getting into the places he'd shown them. IQ managed a thin smile. "His name's Bond—James Bond *Jr.* Have you seen him?"

"The Bond kid?" the first thug asked. Then, to the other man: "He's with the Bond kid. Burn him!"

Both men fired their laser guns. IQ held up a mirror and shut his eyes.

The beams hit the mirror. One bounced off to the right, the other to the left. Gordo and Phoebe held their own mirrors ready, and each one reflected a single beam right back at the two thugs. Hit by their own laser beams, both guards were knocked cold in a second.

"Radical!" Gordo said happily.

"I told you that optics and trigonometry were interesting subjects," IQ told him, opening his eyes again. "I worked out those angles exactly."

"Well done," Phoebe said. "Now, let's look in the van."

The three of them went around to the back of it. They stared in silence into the emptiness. Then they shook their heads and returned to the Warfield Academy van with long faces.

"They must be on that plane," IQ said, breaking the long silence.

"With that ultraheavy Jaws dude," Gordo added.

"In trouble," finished Phoebe. "Could things get worse?"

At that moment, they heard the sound of a plane headed their way. Phoebe grabbed at a pair of binoculars from the box Gordo had packed. "Maybe James has taken over the plane, and it's coming back!" she said, excited.

Gordo grinned. "That's my man!" When Phoebe didn't say anything, he asked: "Does James have things under total control?"

Phoebe bit her lip and handed him the binoculars. Gordo looked upward and saw the plane in a nosedive for the ground.

"I don't think *anyone* has that plane under control," she said shakily, and looked ready to cry. "They're going down!"

In the cabin of the plane, the pilot finally managed to shove Jaws off him. When he saw the ground coming up fast through the cockpit window, he grabbed for the controls. Then he pulled back on them, and the plane began to even out again. It had been a very narrow escape. The plane was only a few hundred feet in the air now, and much too close to the jagged cliffs below. The pilot fought to pull the nose up higher again.

Scumlord had been thrown out of his seat as the plane plummeted. Now he managed to get to his feet again. Facing the shaken Jaws, he yelled: "What happened?"

"It's that young Bond," Jaws said, standing up. "He got loose."

"Well, take care of him!" Scumlord shouted. "That's what I'm paying you for, you idiot!"

"Don't worry, boss," Jaws growled. "I'm going to fix him!" He was really angry now. He tore into the cargo bay. By the time he was finished, you'd need a microscope to see what was left of Bond.

It had been a bad few minutes for James and Tracy when the plane had fallen. The Aston Martin had been thrown forward, and Tracy had fallen onto James. He pushed her off with a smile.

"We can't go on meeting like this," he told her. "People will start talking."

"Aren't you ever serious?" Tracy yelled. "What's happening to the plane?"

"At a guess," James said, "we may be in for a rough landing."

Then the plane straightened out. James backed as far down the cargo bay as he could, and waited. He knew Jaws would be back.

A moment later, the door to the cabin burst open and Jaws stepped through. His eyes were on fire, and he was grinding his metal teeth together, sending off bright sparks. They could hear the noise even over the sound of the car engine. Jaws reached out and hit the button that opened the cargo doors.

"He's not looking very happy," James said.

"Well, I'm not singing for joy myself," Tracy replied. "Now what do we do?"

James smiled and started the car forward again, as fast as it would go.

Jaws didn't move this time. Instead, he stood still, feet apart, hands reaching forward as the car slammed into him.

He shook, but it was the car that stopped. The hood was dented, and steam was rising from under it.

"James!" Tracy yelled. "It didn't even hurt him."

"It must have," James replied. "Perhaps he's just not the sort of person who lets his feelings show."

With a scream of rage, Jaws bent down and grabbed the front of the Aston Martin. He grunted, lifted the wheels into the air, and started pushing the car toward the open doors. Tracy and James were thrown back in their seats. With his face now almost in the grille, Jaws opened his mouth and bit down on the metal.

Inside the car, they heard the squeal of tearing metal and saw Jaws take a huge bite out of the hood. Jaws shook his head wildly as he chewed the metal. He grinned and opened his mouth for another bite. Tracy shrieked in terror, unable to contain her panic any longer.

"James—I think we're next!" she said in a panicked voice.

"Maybe he'll fill up on the car," James said. "He might not have room for dessert."

"I wouldn't bet on it," Tracy replied. "Do something!"

James studied the control panel. Were any of the gadgets still working? Well, there was one way to find out. He hit the button marked LASER BEAM; nothing happened. Well, that one was dead—and so would he and Tracy be if one of the gadgets didn't work! He tried a button marked RAM ROD.

As Jaws chomped off another piece of the car, he stopped and frowned. The grille had opened up with a whir. He looked into the opening, and then something shot out of it, punching him right in the mouth.

Roaring, Jaws dropped the car and fell back into the cockpit door again—

—and right back into the pilot. The pilot fell forward and the plane dropped into a dive.

As the car dropped, James and Tracy were thrown about again. James pushed Tracy off him. "Are you all right?" he asked her.

"Shaken, but not stirred," she managed to joke. "And I'm starting to dislike your driving."

"I'm not too happy with it myself," James told her. "And I don't like this airline much. Why don't we take a later flight?"

He opened the door and jumped out of the Aston Martin. Tracy joined him as he raced for the small side door of the cargo hold. There was a rack of tools beside it, and a single parachute. With one eye on the door to the cabin, he pulled on the parachute.

Tracy, white-faced, said: "But there's only one! What about me?"

James told her: "You'll have to share with me. It should be strong enough for two." *It better be,* James said to himself.

"Won't they just chase us?" Tracy asked. "They must have more parachutes in the cabin, and they could just follow us in the plane."

"I don't think it's us they're after. That goon wouldn't have tried pushing us out of the plane if it was. But they'll be too busy to bother with us anyway." James said. He took IQ's tracking device from his pocket. "IQ said that this could control the Aston Martin. Let's hope he was right." He switched on the device and started to play with the buttons.

The car rolled forward. James hit a second button. The car stopped, then went into reverse. James hit all of the buttons together, and the car started to swerve around as if it were drunk.

"That should liven the party up a bit," James said. Then he opened the side door.

The rush of air grabbed at Tracy. She screamed and held on to James. With a smile, he yelled: "Geronimo!"—and jumped.

Chapter Fourteen
Down, But Not Out

Tracy shrieked as she saw how far up in the air they were. She grabbed James as tight as she could, and was happy to feel his arms holding on to her. Then he pulled the cord, and the parachute opened up. There was a sharp tug, and they started to drift slowly to the ground.

"So do you like hanging around with me?" James asked her.

"Believe me," she said, "at this moment, there's nothing I'd rather do!"

He smiled.

Tracy looked down and closed her eyes. "Just make sure you hold on to me!"

They watched together as the S.C.U.M. jet passed by them on its way back to the ground.

* * *

Inside the plane, everyone was panicking. When Jaws had banged into the pilot, he had also smashed some of the instruments.

"We're going to crash!" the pilot yelled, and jumped out of his seat. He grabbed a parachute from the supply locker, then ran into the cargo bay as he struggled to pull it on.

Scumlord and the two gunmen took one look out of the window and followed him. Scuzzball, who had slept through the entire flight, scampered after them.

By the time Jaws got to his feet, there was nobody else in the cabin. And when he looked in the supply locker, there were no more parachutes left. "Hey!" he yelled. "What about me?"

Scumlord had his parachute on and was trying to avoid being run down by the Aston Martin. The car was running in odd patterns around the cargo bay. The crime boss glared back at Jaws. "This is all your fault!" he yelled. "I don't care what you do!" Then, holding on tight to Scuzzball, he jumped out of the door.

Jaws ran back to the cockpit. The plane was in a free-fall. Jaws grabbed the big control stick and pulled back as hard as he could. It came off in his hands. "Uh-oh," he said. There was no way to fly the plane at all now.

He climbed his way back to the cargo bay—it was straight uphill. The Aston Martin almost hit him, but he made it to the escape door. Then he stood there, looking out. It was certain death to stay on the plane—but did he dare jump out without a parachute?

What else could he do? He closed his eyes and jumped.

Phoebe, Gordo, and IQ were watching the plane as it went into the second dive. It was almost directly over the old airfield again. They didn't know why, but there was obviously a struggle going on on board. It could only mean one thing—the pilot was in trouble.

"James has got them so confused, they don't know if they're coming or going," IQ said. "I hope he gets out before that plane crashes."

"Someone's bailed out!" Phoebe told them, pointing.

They saw a single parachute open up. Phoebe pointed the binoculars at it. "That's either one very fat guy," she said, "or else . . ." Then she saw who it was. "James and Tracy!"

"My main dude, James!" Gordo said.

IQ watched how the parachute was falling. "They're going to land about a mile away," he worked out. "We better go meet them in the van."

"Right," Phoebe agreed. She wouldn't mind seeing James again.

The plane came screaming out of the sky and slammed into the ground in the middle of the old airfield. In a huge ball of fire, it exploded. Blazing bits of wreckage showered all over the area.

Scumlord had just landed safely, and let go of Scuzzball. Then the explosion knocked him off his feet into a huge puddle of mud. He spluttered and managed to get his face out, only to smell smoke —very close. He felt hot.

A piece of wreckage had set his trousers on fire!

With a yell of pain, he sat down in the mud to put the flames out. Filthy, charred, and furious, he watched the plane burning in the middle of the field. Scuzzball started to bounce up and down in the mud, thinking this was a fine new game his master had invented. With a scream, Scumlord held his fist up in the air.

"I almost had this country begging for mercy!" he yelled. "And you ruined it, young Bond! You just wait—I'll get you in my grasp again! And then it'll be you that will beg for mercy!"

Jaws plummeted through the air. He was heading for a small farm. He opened his eyes just in time to see the roof of a barn. The wood shattered, and he fell right through it—right into a huge stack of hay.

The hay broke his fall, but he was still almost knocked out. When he could see again, he realized that there was a chicken standing on his chest, clucking angrily at him.

Jaws felt something warm and sticky oozing into his back. Ugh! Could it be blood? Maybe this time he'd finally, truly hurt himself. He thought grimly about what a terrible day it had been so far. Outwitted by that stupid Bond brat! Falling out of a plane without a parachute! Now this.

Jaws prided himself on his indestructibility. Any kind of injury was an insult, and this seemed like it might be really bad. Gingerly he felt the sticky stuff.

Now he really saw red, and it wasn't because he was looking at blood. It was because he was insanely angry. He'd landed in a chicken nest. The stuff all over his clothes was smashed eggs. This was the last outrage.

Pushing the clucking bird away, Jaws got to his feet. He stood there, swaying, dripping eggs and hay all over. He stared hard at the hole in the roof he'd made. "I'm gonna get that Bond kid for this!" he promised. The chicken was still clucking away at him. Jaws opened his mouth and hissed at the chicken.

It took one look at him and shot, screaming, out of the barn. It made Jaws feel at least a little bit better.

Tracy and James hit the ground gently and rolled over. The white cloth of the parachute fell on top of them, covering them completely. Tracy realized she still had her arms around James, and that he had his around her. Not a bad position to be in . . . and it was quiet here.

"Well," he said with a smile, "peace and quiet at last."

"Finally," she agreed. "And there's something I want you to know."

"What's that?" he asked.

Before Tracy could answer, there was a noise of feet, and then the edge of the parachute was pulled up. Phoebe glared in at them. "Hi, guys," she said. "Are we interrupting something?"

Another edge was lifted, and IQ grinned in at them. "I'll bet you're glad to see us, aren't you?"

James gave a deep sigh. He really wouldn't have minded a bit more time alone with Tracy. Still, he should be glad to have such good and loyal friends. He pulled off the parachute pack. Tracy wriggled out from underneath and got to her feet. Gordo was in the Warfield Academy van nearby in the road.

"Need a lift?" he called.

James shook his head sadly. Then he smiled at Phoebe. "Like I said, you're all heart."

"I know," she said, gazing up at him. "And it's full of love."

Tracy raised an eyebrow. "Maybe we should leave the two of you together under the parachute," she suggested.

"Would you?" asked Phoebe.

James shot Tracy a look. "I wouldn't want you to get a bad reputation," he said quickly.

Happy, Phoebe smiled up at him. "Oh, I'm willing to chance it."

"But I'm not," James said, to himself. It was one thing to face Jaws—and quite another to face Phoebe Farragut!

Chapter Fifteen
What's Going On?

Mr. Milbanks was in the music room, relaxing. He really enjoyed his job, but the pressure sometimes got to him. Then he enjoyed nothing as much as relaxing and listening to his favorite music. Right now, he had Mozart's "Piano Concerto No. 27" on the stereo. It was so peaceful. . . .

"Mr. Milbanks! Sir!"

The headmaster jumped to his feet and looked around for the person that the loud voice belonged to. Then he saw Trevor Noseworthy and groaned. The boy was a real problem. And after what the little troublemaker had pulled on him earlier . . . "What is it, Noseworthy?" he growled.

"Sir, it's James Bond Jr." Trevor couldn't keep the happiness out of his voice. "He's gone against your orders, sir, and left the school."

Bond again? Was there something that

Noseworthy had against him? But he didn't dare take the chance. Mr. Milbanks switched off the CD player. He'd seen too many schools ruined when just one boy broke the rules openly. It set a very bad example to the rest of the students.

"You had better be right about this," he told Trevor. "Nobody breaks into my Mozart without a good reason."

"Oh, I am sure," Trevor said. "Bond has gone."

"Well," the headmaster promised, "if he has indeed broken the rules, then he'll find himself in detention permanently!"

Trevor ran along, leading the way to the boys' dorm and up the stairs to the room Bond and IQ shared together. With a broad grin on his face, Trevor threw open the door and said: "There! Just like I said!"

James looked up from his desk and frowned. "Did you want something, Trevor?" he asked. He had a book open in front of him. Seeing the headmaster, James stood up politely. "Oh, hello, sir. Just getting a little ahead in my classwork. I'm trying to use my detention time wisely."

Trevor stood there, his jaw dropped open, spluttering wildly.

Mr. Milbanks nodded at James. "Good to see you studying, Bond. Don't let me interrupt you." He closed the door, then turned to Trevor, furious. "Noseworthy, I can see I have to teach you to get your facts straight! *You* can spend the rest of the week in detention!"

Trevor's face fell. "But, sir . . ."

The headmaster glared at him. "Would you prefer *two* weeks?"

"Oh no, sir," Trevor said quickly. "One week is fine!"

"Good. Now, I am going back to my room. And I don't want to be disturbed again. For any reason. Is that quite understood?"

"Oh yes, sir," Trevor said. "Very much so." As the headmaster walked off, Trevor turned around to glare at James's door. "I'm going to fix you for this, Bond," he promised. "If it's the last thing I do!"

Inside his room, James gave a sigh of relief. Tracy, Phoebe, Gordo, and IQ came out of the bathroom. "That was a little too close," James said.

"I'll say," IQ agreed. "It's a good thing Mr. Milbanks didn't realize that the book you were studying is open upside down!"

James looked at the book and laughed. "So it is! No wonder I can't remember what I've been studying all day." He looked at his friends. "Well, we're back in one piece, which is something I wasn't sure would happen."

"But what I don't understand," Tracy said, "is what this was all about. Who are those S.C.U.M. people, and why were they so keen on getting hold of you and the Aston Martin?"

James shrugged. "I really don't have any idea," he told her. "But it was kind of fun, wasn't it?"

There was another knock at the door. Phoebe and Tracy started to dive for the bathroom to hide, since it was now past nine P.M. and they weren't supposed to be in the boys' dorm. But the door opened too quickly, and they were caught.

It was Mr. Mitchell. He looked over the guilty faces and frowned. "You do remember that I told you not to have girls in your room after nine," he said to James.

"Yes, sir." James sighed. *Here it comes,* he thought. *More detention. I'll be spending forever in trouble.*

"It's a good thing my eyes have been acting up all day," Mitchell told him. "Otherwise, I might be able to see to the far end of the room."

James sighed again, this time with relief. "I'm sorry to hear that," he said politely.

"I'm sure you are." Mr. Mitchell looked at the five friends. "Well, you've been through a lot today," he said. "I thought you deserved an explanation for it, at the very least."

"That would be nice," Tracy said, then covered her mouth.

Mr. Mitchell smiled. "I didn't hear anything, either. Must be something wrong with my ears, too." He looked at James. "I'm afraid that part of this adventure was my fault. I'm supposed to be retired from the spy game since my cover was blown. But I am still in touch with my old boss—and also your uncle's.

"Well, a group of scientists invented a machine called an electromagnetic pulse generator. It produces a beam of light that can wipe out everything in a computer's memory."

"That's nasty," IQ said. He had a dreamy look in his eyes. "I can see how they might go about it, though. If you take a small—" He broke off and picked up a pad and pen. He spent the rest of Mr. Mitchell's explanation scribbling away.

"Yes," the gym teacher agreed. "And we knew that if anybody heard about the machine, there'd be plenty of interest in it. Double-O-Seven was given the job of delivering the machine to the right people. The E.M.P. was hidden in his new car."

James had a horrible idea of what was coming next.

"Well, it seems S.C.U.M. had intercepted some messages between Double-O-Seven and M," Mr. Mitchell went on. "And they thought that the E.M.P. must be in the Aston Martin. By the time your uncle knew what had happened, it was too late. He was already in the middle of delivering the device, and S.C.U.M. was already after you."

Tracy was shocked. "You mean they put James in danger and they did nothing?" she yelled. "That's horrible!" In her anger she had forgotten that she wasn't even supposed to be there.

"No," the teacher said. "Once they found out that James had arrived here at Warfield, and was in detention, he would be perfectly safe. With the security system here, the enemy agents would just waste their time trying to break in." He gave James a hard look. "What your uncle didn't realize was that you're just like he was at your age, and that you'd managed to skip detention."

Tracy hit herself on the head. "And I was dumb enough to show James the secret way out of the school—and right into trouble!"

Mr. Mitchell smiled. "You couldn't have known what was going on. We kept it hidden from everyone. And, thanks to the five of you, everyone is safe, and the E.M.P. generator has been safely delivered."

"Yes," James agreed sadly. "And the Aston Martin was blown up in the plane crash for nothing. Now I'm stuck here for certain. Great."

The phys ed teacher shrugged. "Sorry about that, James. Now . . ." He looked at Phoebe and Tracy. "I think that these two young ladies that I haven't seen had better return back to their own room." He smiled. "Luckily, I have to go over there. If they were to walk behind me where I can't see them, I don't think that other members of the staff will ask them any difficult questions on the way."

"Yes, sir!" Tracy and Phoebe chorused. Together, all three of them left.

Gordo grinned at James. IQ was still scribbling away on his pad. "Well, James, my man," Gordo said. "I have a totally awesome feeling that this year at the Academy is going to be tubular to the max!"

"Maybe," said James, "if we had a set of wheels." He looked sadly out into the night. "And I blew that part—quite literally!"

Chapter Sixteen
Wheels!

The next day, classes began. James was still unhappy about losing the Aston Martin, and he couldn't pay attention, no matter how he tried. He didn't mind being at Warfield Academy at all—he had made friends with IQ, Gordo, and Phoebe.

And while Mr. Milbanks was a bit too keen on the rules, he seemed like a decent sort of person. As long as he didn't know about any of their . . . after-school activities, things should be fine.

Then there was Mr. Mitchell. There was more to him than met the eye. Was he really just the retired secret agent he claimed to be? He had seemed to be in the know about the generator. And he admitted he still talked to Gordo's father and James's uncle. Was he up to even more than that? James knew he wouldn't ever get straight answers. And he knew that his stay at Warfield was going to be pretty interesting—and busy.

And finally, there was Tracy. James was not ready to settle down with just one girl, but if he was—ever!—then he knew it would be with someone like her. She was just the sort of girl he liked, and he hoped that he'd be able to finally get to know her better.

But without wheels, he'd be stuck in school permanently.

James spent most of the morning thinking of ways he might have saved the Aston Martin. It was such a beautiful car. It was gone all because of S.C.U.M. He had a lot to learn about fighting bad guys.

If he'd been asked, he couldn't have said what the classes were that he sat through. The morning dragged on and on. He just wanted it to be over. Finally, the lunch bell rang, and he went with IQ to the cafeteria. He had no desire to eat, though.

"James! James!"

He looked up and saw Tracy and Phoebe making their way over toward him. Tracy was smiling happily.

"I just had a phone call for you," she said. "There's a package for you from your uncle."

"Not again!" he groaned. "I've had enough of that old trick. This time, I'm staying here. Anyway, I can't get into Sawley to pick it up even if it's real."

"Oh, it's real this time," Phoebe told him, taking his left arm and trying to snuggle in close to him.

"And it's not in Sawley," Tracy added, taking his other arm. She and Phoebe began to drag him out of the cafeteria. "It's here, at school. In the parking lot."

"Silly place to leave a package," James said, frowning.

"Not *this* package," Tracy said.

IQ tagged along, and they walked around the building to the parking lot. There were the cars belonging to the staff that James remembered from yesterday. And, in the middle of the lot, a bright red sports car.

"The package is in the car?" he asked.

"No," Tracy told him. "The package *is* the car."

Hardly able to believe it, James went over to it. It was a wild-looking, low convertible with plush leather bucket seats. He looked inside it. There were a number of extra switches on the dashboard, and a little tag hanging from the rearview mirror. He pulled it off and read it:

"To James from Uncle James. Well done—You're a chip off the old Bond."

James looked up and saw Mr. Mitchell and Gordo approaching. The gym teacher smiled.

"I told Double-O-Seven about the car," he said. "And he seemed to think you deserved a present for fixing those crooks. If it wasn't for your help, he might not have been able to finish his mission."

"Radical wheels, my man!" Gordo added.

"I just *love* that color," Phoebe said.

"It is a very nice car, James," Tracy told him.

IQ's eyes gleamed. "I'll bet my grandfather had something to say when they built it." He touched the dashboard controls. "I wonder what these are all for?"

The key was in the car. James grinned, happy again. "Well, why don't we all find out?"

Mr. Mitchell grabbed the key quickly. "Oh, no," he said. "You're confined to the school all week. Remember?"

James sighed. Then he smiled. A week wasn't *too* long to wait—not with these wheels to dream about! He looked at his friends. "Well, one week from today," he told them, "we're going to find out just what this little beauty can do."

Phoebe almost purred: "Oh, James, I can hardly wait till you take me for a ride."

James sighed. That wasn't what he had meant at all! Then he looked at Tracy. "How about you?" he asked her.

She gave him a grin. "Ask me again in a week."

James nodded. He definitely had a lot to look forward to at Warfield Academy.

Look for these exciting JAMES BOND JR. adventures:

#2 The Eiffel Target The foul Dr. Derange has planted a nuclear bomb in the Eiffel Tower! Can James sneak to Paris and disarm the warhead?

#3 Live and Let's Dance James is in a deadly race against the clock! If he doesn't get to Switzerland in time, the notorious arms dealer Baron von Skarin will assassinate the heir to the throne of Zamora.

#4 Sandblast! The evil Pharaoh Fearo is trying to buy up the world's supply of oil with stolen treasures. If he succeeds, S.C.U.M. will rule the earth.

JAMES BOND JR

Contest Rules
Create Your Own James Bond Jr. Villain

1. Mail all entries to: **James Bond Jr. Contest**, Puffin Books, Penguin USA, 375 Hudson Street, New York, NY 10014. One entry per person. 2. All entries must be received by November 1, 1992. 3. The winning entries will be judged as follows: 50% for drawing, 50% for essay. All entries become property of Danjac and UA Corp. and can be used for promotional purposes. The two winners will be notified by mail. 4. This contest is open to all U.S. and Canadian residents between the ages of 8 and 12 as of December 1, 1991. The winners will be announced on February 1, 1993. 5. Two winners will each receive a Nintendo™ system and a **James Bond Jr.** Game Pak, plus an Espionage Kit and a complete **James Bond Jr.** library. Taxes, if any, are the responsibility of the prize winners. Winners' parents/guardians will be required to sign and return a statement of eligibility. Names and addresses of the winners may be used for promotional purposes. 6. No substitution of prizes is permitted. 7. For the name of the prize-winners, send a self-addressed, stamped envelope to: **James Bond Jr. Contest,** Puffin Books Marketing Dept., Penguin USA, 375 Hudson Street, New York, NY 10014.

The James Bond Jr. Create a Villain Contest

Puffin is pleased to announce the **James Bond Jr.** contest that could win you a Nintendo™ system and a **James Bond Jr.** Game Pak, plus an Espionage Kit and a complete **James Bond Jr.** library!

Being 007's nephew is glamorous, all right, but it also means running up against some pretty unsavory characters. Submit a drawing plus a 200 word or less essay describing the most despicable, low-down bounder ever to disgrace the world of espionage. Please submit your drawing and essay on two separate sheets of white 8 1/2 x 11 paper, and make sure your essay is neatly printed or typewritten. Fill out this coupon completely and staple it to your entry.

Mail your entry to: **James Bond Jr. Contest**
Puffin Books Marketing Dept.
Penguin USA
375 Hudson St.
New York, NY 10014

Name ______________________________ Age __________

Address ______________________________________

City/State/Zip ___________________________________

Store name (where you saw offer) ____________________

Store address ___________________________________

City/State/Zip ___________________________________